SCORCHED EARTH

For Erin,
my best and strongest ally against the darkness.

BOOK TWO OF
THE DARK MATTER SERIES

SCORCHED
EARTH

CLAYTON SMITH

PROLOGUE

Leonard shuffled to his front door. His knees ached, his ankles cracked with every step, and his grip on the knob of his cane wasn't as strong as it used to be. Walking wasn't just a physical challenge these days; it was a mental one, too. Cataracts had blurred his vision, and he couldn't trust his own view of the floor in front of him, which softened and swayed and seemed to be constantly shifting under his feet.

His back was stooped from calcium deficiency. His knuckles were inflamed with rheumatism. His scalp was threaded with wispy white hairs. His teeth were made of resin and wires. His skin was covered with liver spots, and his fingernails were brittle and yellow. His chin bore a scar from when he had fallen two months ago and cracked it on the edge of the countertop.

He grumbled under his breath as he eased himself across the foyer. Why couldn't they let him watch TV in peace?

The doorbell rang again, for the fourth time since Leonard had struggled out of his recliner. "Yeah, yeah, I hear you," he yelled, and the effort of making his voice so loud dislodged a knob of phlegm from his throat, and he coughed and hacked and almost choked to death right there on the spot.

By the time he opened the door, he was trembling with exhaustion.

"What do you want?" he asked, squinting out into the overcast day.

The woman standing on his porch was dressed in a long, purple cloak with a deep hood pulled up over her head. The fabric hung down and obscured her eyes. A small purple pendant hung around her neck on a thin gold chain, and she wore golden silk gloves that went all the way up past her wrists and disappeared into the sleeves of her cloak. In her hands, she held a purple envelope that bore a golden wax seal.

She didn't speak. She simply held the envelope out to Leonard.

"What's this, Halloween?" the old man muttered, glaring at the woman's robe. He glanced suspiciously at the envelope, and when it became clear that she wouldn't speak or leave the porch until he took it, he swiped the sealed message with a trembling hand. "Go back to Toon Town," he grumped, turning back into his house and slamming the door behind him.

He whispered angrily to himself in the foyer, curses, mostly, about being interrupted during his television show, and about the fashion choices of young people these days. But soon the annoyance drained away, and he was left with guilt. He sighed, and this caused another coughing fit. He doubled over and hacked away for a few seconds, then recovered and wiped his mouth with the sleeve of his sweater. He turned back and opened the door again.

The woman on the porch was gone.

He stepped outside and looked down the street to the left. He looked to the right. Even though he had clear views down to both ends of the block, there was no sign of the woman.

"Hmpf," he said, retreating back into the gloom of his house.

He carried the envelope over to his recliner, and he moaned in pain as his hips worked hard to lower him down on shaky legs. He finally collapsed into the upholstery, wheezing hard, out of breath. He picked up his glasses from the tray table that was propped up next to the chair. Even with the glasses on, it took him a few hard blinks before the envelope came into focus. There was no writing on it—no name, no address, nothing. Just the golden seal on back.

He couldn't see well enough to make out the intricacies of the seal, but he doubted he would have recognized it even if he had a clear view. He didn't know anyone fancy enough for all that hoity-toity rigmarole.

He stuffed his thumb up under the paper and tore open the flap. There was a stiff piece of heavy-stock paper inside. He drew it out and held it up to the lamp so he could get a good look.

Leonard's eyes grew wide. He brought the piece of cardstock closer to his nose to get a better look. He verified the text on the paper.

He looked up.

He took off his glasses.

He curled his lips into a nasty grin.

CHAPTER 1

"This place is great...we'll take it!"

Virgil stood next to Simon on the sidewalk, beaming at the structure in front of them. He wondered if he had ever seen anything so beautiful in his entire life.

Simon, on the other hand, was absolutely positive he had never seen anything worse. "Virgil. This is a bounce house."

Virgil scoffed. "It's an inflatable amusement and social structure."

"It's a bounce house."

"So what?"

"So we're not making a bounce house the official office of Dark Matter Investigations!"

"Why not?!" Virgil cried, throwing up his hands and stomping around in a circle, just to show his frustration. He had spent the last four days scouring all of Templar for the perfect office location, and he had decided definitively that the inflatable amusement and social structure was the perfect home for their new business.

Simon rubbed fiercely at his temples. "Well, Virg, for starters, it doesn't have a roof."

"It's an open-air concept!"

"For another, there are no doors."

"That's a *good* thing! It shows our rock-solid trust in our fellow community members!" Virgil insisted.

"We track down people from our community who call demons forth from hell so they can peel the flesh from every human being in the city; we don't *have* rock-solid trust in our fellow community members!"

Virgil crossed his arms. "Not with that attitude, we don't."

"Virgil. It's a bounce house. There are probably more than one thousand very good reasons why we can't use it as our office." Simon turned to face the bright yellow inflatable castle. It rocked lazily in the autumn breeze. "And also, why is there even a fully-inflated bounce house in a parking lot with a 'for rent' sign taped to the outside of it?!"

"Because the bright young entrepreneurs at the Pounce Trounce Bounce House Emporium decided to set it up and rent it out as a workspace as a promotional gimmick," Virgil explained. "Do you know what that means?"

"That Pounce Trounce Bounce House Emporium is going to go out of business in about eight minutes?" Simon guessed.

"That the rent on this place is a *steal!*"

Simon shook his head. He turned without saying a word and headed back to the Pontiac 6000LE, parked at the edge of the bounce house's lot.

"Hey! Where are you going?" Virgil asked, trotting after him.

Simon pulled open the door. "I'm going to see our office. Our *actual* office. And with any luck, it'll come stocked with a brand new business partner." He got into the car and closed the door.

Virgil ran around to the passenger side and jumped in just as Simon was turning the key. "You got us a different office?"

"Calling it a *different* office implies that this place is also an office, and I want to be very clear that it is not. But yes, I found us an office." He pulled away from the bounce house and headed toward the Highlands neighborhood, just east of downtown Templar.

"*You've* been looking for an office?" Virgil asked, confused.

"Yep."

Virgil furrowed his brow. "Then why did you have *me* looking for an office?"

"I didn't have you looking for an office, Virgil. I had you running an errand that I knew you would be terrible at so I could get you out of my hair long enough for me to find us an actual office."

Virgil's mouth hung open. He turned slowly and stared out at the road. He sat back in his seat. "*Well*," he said, sounding affronted. Then he considered it for a second. His face brightened. "You know, from a business perspective, I guess that was actually a really solid plan."

"Thank you."

"I should *not* be in charge of important things like picking out the office."

"I'm aware."

"I should be in charge of what sort of snacks we keep in the kitchen."

"There's no kitchen," Simon pointed out. "But yes, you can pick the snacks."

They drove on until they hit the Highlands. Virgil hadn't spent much time in that part of town, and he looked with interest at the strip malls and fast food joints that flashed by them as they cruised down the mostly-empty street. "Not a lot of foot traffic," he pointed out.

"It's Saturday. I'm sure it picks up during the work week. Besides, it doesn't matter. We're not a convenience store. We're a highly-specialized investigation company. People will seek us out."

Virgil continued to gaze around the area. "There are no street signs anywhere," he said.

"Yeah, I noticed that too."

"We're going to be hard to find."

"We'll be fine."

"Simon—"

"Virgil, we'll be fine!" Simon cut him off, annoyed.

"But Simon—"

"Virgil! It's fine!"

"Okay," Virgil shouted, "but there is a giant lizard creature about to eat that guy's face off over there, and I think maybe we should go and stop him."

Simon peered out the window in the direction Virgil was pointing. "Oh," he said, noticing the man who was struggling with a half-man, half-lizard mutant over in front of the Church's Chicken. He veered into the parking lot and threw the Pontiac into park. "Well, you could have just said so."

Virgil rolled his eyes. "We're going to be great at being business partners," he said sarcastically.

Then he pulled Gladys, the mystical curiocus Skee-Ball ball, out of his psychic vault and charged the mutant lizard.

CHAPTER 2

He wasn't the first lizard-creature they had ever seen, but he was definitely the biggest.

Every inch of his green, scaly body was covered with muscle. His huge, bulging arms connected to a pair of meaty shoulders that were about as wide as the Pontiac. He had big, powerful hands that looked like they belonged to a professional football player. His lizard head was long and serpentine, with black, intelligent eyes. He had a thick green tail that waved through the air and a forked red tongue that slithered out between his reptilian lips as he towered over the terrified, blubbering man, whom the lizard had knocked to the ground.

The lizard-thing was wearing clothes, thank goodness— not all of them did—but his shirtsleeves were ripped along the seams, and his pant legs were completely shredded. That could only mean one thing.

"Hey! Werelizard!" Virgil called, giving a loud whistle. "Why don't you pick on someone your own size?"

The creature jerked his head to the side, noticing Simon and Virgil for the first time. He sized them up with a quick, jerky movement of his head. "The two of you put together are sssssmaller than he isss."

Virgil's shoulders slumped dejectedly. "I *told* you we need to start going to the gym," he said to Simon.

"Not the time," Simon reminded him.

"Oh. Right."

Simon pushed up his left sleeve, revealing the dark gray manacle that he wore around his wrist. He gave it a shake, and it instantly lit up with a deep orange glow. "We don't want to hurt you," he said. "We want to help you."

The lizard laughed, a wet, hissing rattle that scraped up from the back of his throat. "Help me?" he said. He turned away from the fallen man completely and faced the two novice magicians. He raised his arms into the air and looked at them admiringly. "Help me with what? I've reached the top of the evolutionary ladder."

"We're all going to evolve into lizards?" Virgil asked suspiciously. "So much for my social calendar."

"You don't have a social calendar," Simon said.

"And if I become a lizard, I'll *never* have one."

"Good point," Simon said. He hadn't taken his eyes off the creature for a second. He closed his right hand and whispered some words in Latin. A white light began to glow between the cracks in his fingers.

"What's that?" Virgil murmured out of the side of his mouth, trying not to take his eyes off the werelizard either, but intensely curious about Simon's new trick.

"Cacophony spell. Weren't you paying attention last week?"

"No, not really," Virgil admitted.

"We have to get him away from the victim." The man who had been attacked by the lizard-creature was still cowering on the ground, shaking with fear beneath the swishing tail of the mutant.

"I don't think that's going to be a problem," Virgil observed.

The lizard-thing had focused his entire attention on the pair of them, seemingly forgetting about his victim altogether. The creature took another step toward them, his reptilian feet hitting the pavement with such power and force that each step cracked the blacktop. He seemed to increase in size even as they watched. "You thought you would be heroessss," the lizard spat. "How upsssetting to learn that you'll be just a sssnack insss-stead." He spat at Virgil, a huge, lime-green mucous blob that sailed through the air, heading toward his face. Virgil jumped out of the way, and the spitball missed his head, but it nicked the top of his left shoulder. He screamed in pain; the lizard's mucous was highly acidic, and it had burned through the fabric of his shirt and seared a shallow channel in his skin.

"Ow! Come on!" Virgil hollered, winding up his shoulder to try to shake off the pain. "That hurt, *and* it was super gross!"

"Look," Simon said, trying to gain some semblance of control on the situation, "we know this isn't you. This isn't who you are. The real you is in there somewhere, and probably scared." He leapt to the side to avoid a flying spitball. It struck the tire of a pickup truck behind him, and the tire burst, melting into a liquid-rubber puddle.

Simon struggled to maintain his focus. "We can help you. We know someone who can lift your curse."

"My curssssse is ssspending mosssst of my life asssss a man," the werelizard hissed. He took another two steps toward them, and Simon decided that was far enough away from the victim. He opened his right hand and hurled the ball of white light across the parking lot, just to the left of the werelizard. The light exploded in mid-air, and it burst out with the incredibly loud, discordant sounds of cymbals crashing, trumpets blaring, and saxophones wailing. The lizard-creature clapped his hands over his ears and darted away from the sound, moving himself into the middle of the parking lot, away from the victim, and away from the windows of the Church's Chicken.

"Now!" Simon cried. He fired his manacle, and the brilliant orange energy bullet tore through the air and ripped through the lizard's right shoulder. The monster howled with pain. Virgil gripped Gladys, wound up, and let loose. The wooden ball zoomed toward the lizard, picking up speed as it went, and it struck the same shoulder that Simon had just blasted a hole through.

But maybe Virgil had thrown Gladys a little *too* hard, because the ball exploded right through the werelizard's shoulder, completely severing the arm.

"Oh," Virgil said, straightening up. The blood drained from his face, leaving him pale. He clamped a hand over his mouth. "I think I'm going to be sick," he said.

"Well *that* was surprising," Simon agreed.

The lizard's snout frothed with rage. He glared down at his detached arm, lying useless on the ground. Then he reared back, lifted his head, and roared, like a wolf howling at the moon. As he screamed, the stump beneath his shoulder began to bubble up, as if it were growing boils. The boils pushed out and became *fingers*…the fingers were followed by a hand, and then a wrist, and then an arm. Simon and Virgil watched in disgusted horror as the werelizard grew another arm to replace the one he'd lost. It was covered in thick, green mucous that dripped down onto the asphalt like viscous rain as the arm grew to full size.

The lizard stopped roaring. He looked down at his new arm, flexing his fingers and his elbow, testing the arm. Satisfied, he reached down with his new hand and picked up his severed arm. Then he turned his attention to Simon and Virgil, and he began to approach.

"Nope, nope, nope, nope, nope," Virgil said, throwing up a kinesthetic shield in each hand and stumbling backward, away from the advancing monster. But Simon was frozen with fear and a certain amount of nauseated awe; his brain couldn't convince his legs to move. He watched open-mouthed as the lizard approached. The monster drew himself up to his full height, then he lifted his detached arm and brought it down across Simon's head, using it as a club to bash his temple.

Simon stumbled a few steps, then fell to the ground.

"Hey!" Virgil shouted. "Don't hit my friend with your lopped-off arm, you—" But he didn't get to finish his sentence, because the lizard hurled the arm at him next. He ducked behind his shields, and they deflected the lifeless arm easily. Virgil watched it bounce off the vibrant orange surface of the magic shield and roll onto the blacktop. "Heh," he said, having proudly survived the same attack that Simon hadn't been able to fend off. He lifted his eyes to gloat a little, and when he did, he saw the lizard-creature charging.

"Whoa!" Virgil cried, taking cover behind his shields.

The werelizard rammed into him with one huge fist, cracking both shields in half. The force of the impact knocked Virgil back, and he fell onto the ground. His shields had dissolved after cracking, and he held up his hands, willing them back into being. But they seemed a little gun-shy after the lizard's attack; a small shower of sparks shot out of each hand, but nothing more. The shields wouldn't form.

"Aw, come on...not now," Virgil whined, shaking his hands and trying to coax the magic out.

Simon struggled to one foot. He held the side of his face; a bruise was already forming above his cheek. He moved his jaw to make sure it still worked. It did, but not without a considerable amount of pain.

He got his other foot under him and straightened up. He turned to face the lizard.

The monster flicked his heavy tail, hard. It caught Simon in the ribs, and he went back down.

The werelizard approached Virgil again, murder reflecting from his wet, black eyes. Virgil abandoned the failing shields and reached out for Gladys. The wooden ball zoomed back toward him from across the lot. Just as it approached, the lizard reached out his left hand without looking and snatched it out of the air. Gladys worked hard to break free, yanking the lizard's arm back and forth, but the creature held it tightly and wouldn't let it escape.

Virgil only had one play left. He had left his manacle in the car, but he didn't need it at this range. He closed up his right hand into a fist and felt the burning magic fill it from his gut. It filled his hand with light. He held up the fist and opened it, grunting with the effort of pushing out every ounce of magic he could muster.

But as soon as the spark left his hand, it evaporated into the air, dissolving in a puff of steam, and doing absolutely zero damage to the oncoming monster.

"You've got to be kidding me," Virgil muttered.

Simon was still on his hands and knees, grasping his side and taking labored, measured breaths. The werelizard was upon Virgil now, towering above him. The monster cracked his knuckles, and his tongue shot out and ran a lap around his lips. "I hope you hate thissss asss much assss I'm going to enjoy it," the lizard said. Then he raised both fists high in the air and brought them screaming down at Virgil's head.

Virgil closed his eyes and waited for the impact.

But the impact didn't come.

He heard the werelizard give a soft whimper. Virgil cracked open one eyelid and peeked out. The lizard was shrinking, his muscles deflating and losing their green hue. His scales spread out, connected, and smoothed over until they were just skin. His long snout pushed back in on itself and melted into a nose; his black eyes shrank in a pool of blue, and just like that, the creature had irises in his eyes.

The werelizard had transformed back into a human man.

He was older, probably in his forties, with gray lines streaking through his brown hair. He was small, too, scrawny; he was probably taller than Virgil and Simon both, but skinner than either of them.

He crumpled to the ground, the ends of his ripped, tattered clothes fluttering out over his arms and legs.

Behind him, standing with a mixed look of annoyance and pride on her face, was Abby.

"You can send one of the most powerful demons in history back to hell, but you can't take down a herpetomorph?"

Virgil blinked up at her. "What's a herpetomorph?"

Abby walked around the crumpled man and reached down. She took Virgil's hand and helped him to his feet. "A man who morphs into a lizard."

"Oh, you mean a werelizard."

"They're called herpetomorphs," she said.

Virgil looked down at the man with disgust. "Ew, he changes into herpes too?"

Abby rolled her eyes. Magnified as they were by her glasses, the effect was pretty impressive. "No, idiot. Lizards are herptiles. The study of lizards is herpetology. Someone who changes into a lizard is a herpetomorph."

Virgil squinted at her. "Sounds like herpes," he said.

Abby sighed and walked away to go check on Simon. Virgil looked down and visually inspected the herpetomorph. "Hey," he said, nudging the man with his toe. "You dead?"

The man groaned, but didn't get up.

Abby slipped her glove back onto her hand, reached down, and grabbed Simon's arm. "You okay?" she asked, helping him to his feet.

"I don't think anything's broken," he replied, holding his side and wincing. His cheek was swollen, and his ribs probably would be too, for a while, but otherwise he was okay. "How'd you do that?" he asked.

"I found his humanity, and I reflected it back to him," she said casually, as if it were the simplest thing in the world.

"I thought that's how you scrambled people's brains."

"That's if I close a continuous empathetic loop. I only sent the herpetomorph's empathy back once."

Simon nodded and pretended to understand. "Mm," he said.

"He turns into herpes," Virgil explained happily, hearing Abby say his new favorite word again. "I think he's coming to."

Simon and Abby joined Virgil, and the three of them stood over the thin man on the ground. He groaned, and he blinked groggily as he struggled to open his eyes against the sun. "Where—what happened?" he asked. He looked down at his ripped shirt and his torn pants. Then his head drooped, and he rubbed his temples with his thumbs. "Not again," he muttered.

"It's okay," Abby said, crouching down and speaking softly. "You didn't hurt anyone. Not here, anyway."

"*I'm* pretty hurt," Simon pouted, but Abby shot daggers in his direction, and he closed his mouth. She had empathized with the herpetomorph, and while the lizard-monster was a vicious, cruel beast, the human inside was kind and good-natured, and heavy with guilt over his counterpart's destructive, sometimes murderous actions.

"Come back and see us once a month," Abby said. "I think I can help you keep the lizard at bay." She reached into her back pocket, retrieved a business card, and handed it over to him.

"'Dark Matter Investigations,'" he read out loud. "'Simon Dark and Virgil Matter. Heroes of Templar. Defeaters of Evil. Practitioners of Kinesthetic Magic.'" He looked up at them, confused. "What is this?"

"It sounds kind of dorky when you hear it out loud like that," Simon frowned.

Virgil slugged him on his shoulder. "Are you kidding me? It sounds *awesome!*" he beamed.

Abby ignored them both and directed her words at the herpetomorph. "We take care of hexes, curses, and black magic transformations. Give us a call to set up an appointment; we'll float your goodness to the top and keep the lizard buried. Cool?"

The man looked startled, as if he had been in a dark closet and someone had just turned on the lights, but he nodded, and he tucked the business card into his pocket. "Thank you," he said quietly. He struggled to his feet with Abby's help. "Thank you," he said again, more forcefully, looking her in the eye. Then he looked around, dazed and disoriented, and shambled across the parking lot and around the corner of the building, shaking out his right arm and flexing his fingers, as if they felt somehow alien to the rest of his body.

Virgil smiled confidently as he watched the man go. "I don't want to come off like a braggart, but man. We are *good* at this."

"Well, Abby's good at this," Simon pointed out, rubbing his cheek.

"Hey, we didn't die," Virgil pointed out. "That's pretty good."

"Thanks for the help," Simon said to Abby, blushing.

"You guys are lucky I was so close."

"Yeah, about that," Virgil said suspiciously, rubbing his chin, "what *are* you doing here?"

"I was at the office, and I saw you dummies get outmatched from across the street."

"Our office is across the street?" Virgil asked, spinning around and craning his neck at the line of buildings across the road. "Where?"

Simon stepped up and put a hand on his friend's shoulder. He pointed proudly to a unit at the end of a strip mall on the far side of the block. "That," he said happily, "is the new home of Dark Matter."

Virgil's eyes locked on his new office. His smile faded. His heart sank.

"You have got to be kidding me," he said.

CHAPTER 3

"Come on, Virg! Isn't it great?"

Virgil looked around the room. He wasn't feeling Simon's excitement. "I don't think 'great' is the first word that comes to mind…"

In fact, the first word that came to Virgil's mind was "laundry." The room was filled with about two dozen washing machines and clothes dryers, and there was a faded yellow sign hanging above the door that read SOAPS 'N SUDS.

"This isn't an office. This is a laundromat."

"It *was* a laundromat," Simon corrected him, still sounding excited for reasons that Virgil couldn't quite put his finger on. "But *now* it's an office!" He sauntered out to the middle of the room and spread his arms wide. "This'll be great! It's affordable, it's functional. It's just what we need. We'll get some desks, some chairs, we'll hang our own sign…we're in business!"

But Virgil stared at him, incredulous. "Simon! *It's a laundromat.*"

"No, Virgil, it's not!"

"*There are washing machines everywhere.*"

Simon frowned. He had to concede that point. "They're going to be taken out sometime next week. The place just closed a few days ago, and there was a mix-up with the truck. But soon they'll be gone, and we'll have the whole place to ourselves, and hey—in the meantime, they left everything hooked up, so you get free laundry."

Virgil closed his eyes and shook his head. "First of all, it's not free laundry, the machines are coin-operated."

"But we have the keys to the coin boxes, so we're just paying ourselves."

"And also," Virgil said, ignoring him, "unless you're going to drag a laundry bag all the way across town from our apartment instead of doing laundry in the machines we *usually* use in the basement of our own *building*, the only possible clothes I can imagine that you would wash here are the ones that you wear to work. And I am *not* going into business with you if you take clients in your underwear," Virgil said, crossing his arms. "I am *firm* on that point."

"No one's doing anything in their underwear," Abby said, stepping between them. "Virgil, you're right, it's a laundromat, but it's also in your price range."

"The bounce house was in our price range," Virgil muttered.

Abby ignored him and pressed on. "You haven't actually made any money yet, so until you start drumming up some business, this is what you can afford."

"And only because of Llewyn's allowance," Simon added.

Virgil groaned. "I really wish you'd stop calling it an allowance. And you know, we could afford a better place if you put some of that grandpa drive-thru money of yours to work..." His eyes glinted with mischief.

"I need that money to cover *your* half of the rent on our apartment," Simon shot back.

"Hmpf," Virgil grunted. "Fair point."

"So you make do here. For now. And if you want a better building in a better neighborhood, you'd better start handing out some of these." Abby picked up a stack of business cards from the top of one of the washing machines and shoved it into Virgil's hand. "I won't be there every time to do it for you. I have a real job. One that actually gives me a paycheck."

Virgil stuck the cards into his pocket. "All right, all right, leave Squeezy Cheez out of it," he grumbled. He crossed his arms and skulked around the room, inspecting the place. The building was old. *Very* old. The white linoleum on the floor had faded to a sickly yellow, and it was peeling in most places. A few of the tiles had come up altogether, leaving a rough patch of dried mortar showing between the other squares. There were some cabinets near the back, made of a cheap, flimsy wood. They were covered with the tacky residue of decades' worth of laundry detergent spills. The washing machines and dryers themselves looked like they had originally been purchased from a showroom in the 1950s.

Still, it wasn't without its charm…

"We could film a killer horror movie in here," he decided aloud.

"That's the spirit," Simon said cheerfully. "I was going to make it a surprise, but since you've just turned into such a paragon of positivity, I'm going to go ahead and tell you: I took some of my 'grandpa' money and bought us a sign! A *real* sign! I had a professional design it and everything." Simon could hardly contain his pride. His chest puffed out, and the tips of his ears tinged pink. "It should be here on Monday."

Virgil found himself impressed. "Wow. That's really cool, Simon. Thanks for doing that."

"You're welcome," Simon smiled.

"And, look, it comes with a TV," Abby said. She picked up a remote from a table near the wall and clicked on a small television that was propped up on a high shelf suspended from the ceiling by two cheap-looking chains. It was an old TV set, and the screen took a few seconds to warm up after Abby turned it on. Slowly, a fuzzy picture faded into view.

"Yeah, I guess this'll be okay," Virgil decided, completing his inspection of the room. "A couple of rugs, the right *feng shui*, this whole place will…" He stopped talking when he looked at Simon and Abby and realized they were completely ignoring him. They were both staring up at the television, their jaws set in exactly the same hard way. "You guys, what—?" he began. But he didn't finish the question. He didn't need to.

All his questions were answered when he looked up at the horror that was unfolding on live TV.

CHAPTER 4

"Just to be clear, we all saw the same thing, right?" Virgil called out, climbing into the passenger seat of the 6000LE. "My eyes aren't making things up?"

"We saw it," Simon confirmed, sliding in behind the wheel. "I'm not sure I *believe* it, but yeah, we saw it."

"I'll see you guys over there," Abby said, hopping up into her pickup. She tore out of the parking lot, loose asphalt gravel flying from her tires and pelting the dumpster that was parked next to their building. She tore out into the street, took a hard right, and disappeared around the corner.

"Great, now she's going to beat us there, and we'll never hear the end of it," Virgil sighed. Truth be told, it didn't really feel like the right time to be making jokes…but making jokes was a whole lot better than trying to process what he'd seen on TV.

The channel had been set to the local news. In the foreground, the reporter was talking into the camera, trying to maintain her composure, but she kept peeking over her shoulder, and every time she did, she lost track of her words, and dead space filled the airwaves until the people in the studio nudged her and asked her to keep describing what she was seeing.

She was standing in front of the football field at West Templar High School. There were players on the field, high school boys wearing practice jerseys for a weekend scrimmage, probably going over failed plays from the previous night's game. Though to say that they were *on* the field wasn't exactly right. They were actually suspended *above* the field, all three dozen or so of them, floating anywhere from three feet to ten feet above the grass.

Most of the boys were clustered together near the far end of the field, a few yards from the end zone. They must have been working on a goal line play when whatever it was that hit them, hit them.

And the thing that had hit them was still there.

The players were all suspended over the grass, but they weren't just hovering; they had been *lifted* off the field. Each player had a bright tree-branch-sized bolt of lightning through his chest. Each branch zigzagged across the field, extending from the players' torsos and meeting in the center of the field, near the fifty-yard line, joining a massive column of electricity that had shot down from a strange nest of purplish-gold clouds overhead.

The reporter on the television had described what had happened, though she didn't quite seem to believe it. The purple clouds had gathered quickly, and everyone in the surrounding neighborhood had seen them. They were so odd-looking, so unique, that many of the folks near the high school had stepped out of their cars and their houses to marvel at them and get a better look. And as they watched, the center of the clouds opened up, and the bright column of light touched down, as quickly as lightning, striking the football field. But unlike lightning, the column of energy didn't flash, strike, and retreat. This one flashed, struck, and remained in place. Energy from the cloud hummed and vibrated along the column, and then the bolts of lightning shot out from the column, one for each player. The bolts zapped through their pads, shooting through their chests like swords through paper. Once the lightning had run them through, the players' eyes glowed with bright energy, and white light radiated from their fingers. The energy column looked like a thick tree trunk with thirty lightning branches that were heavy with the fruit of light-up humans.

Then the branches raised themselves up, lifting the football players with them, until they were suspended above the ground.

But none of that was the worst part.

The worst part, even though it was hard to tell given the graininess of the television reception, was that the boys who had been impaled by the lightning still seemed to be alive and in an extraordinary amount of pain.

"Quick question," Virgil said as Simon careened around a corner, zooming toward the interstate that would deposit them less than a mile from the high school. "What's our plan, here?"

"I don't know," Simon admitted, tightening his grip on the wheel. The 6000LE flashed past the cars on their right and on their left as Simon weaved in and out of the lanes. "We have to try *something*."

Virgil considered their options. "We could try frying the cloud."

"We could," Simon said. "With all the energy it's forcing down, we might just be making it stronger."

"Yeah," Virgil said quietly.

"Do you think Gladys could interrupt the smaller lightning bolts? Like, if you throw her at one of the branches, do you think it might break the beam?"

"Maybe," Virgil said doubtfully. He pictured the Skee-Ball ball that was sitting in his vault. "I don't know if she can withstand electricity like that. She might burn to a crisp and not make any difference."

"I don't know," Simon said, mostly to himself. "But we have to do something."

He pulled the wheel to the right, and the Pontiac screeched across two lanes of traffic to hit the exit ramp toward West Templar High. They drove the rest of the way in silence, and when they pulled into the parking lot, Abby was there, waiting anxiously.

"Look at that thing," she said, approaching the car as they got out. She turned and pointed at the sky over the football field. "Just *look*."

The energy column looked even more menacing in person than it did on TV. And there was no doubt about it: there was a *constant* energy flow hitting the ground from the strangely-colored clouds up above. They could tell by streaks of blue and white light that flashed down the column, from top to bottom, and by the way the entire pillar sparked and crackled with kinetic power.

They could see the players, too...most of them, anyway. The ones on the far side of the field were hidden by the sheer width of the lightning column, but the ones they *could* see were moving their fingers. The light that shone from them flashed and moved in every direction, putting Simon in mind of a night club he'd snuck into once with his sister, Laura.

Of course, the football players' hands could have been moving on their own from the jolts of energy shooting through their bodies. But Simon knew they were alive.

He knew it because he could hear them screaming.

Simon broke into a run, heading toward the field. "Simon!" Virgil cried after him, but Simon didn't stop, so Virgil hurried to catch up.

"Two points for bravery," Abby sighed, "and negative ten for running headlong into their own deaths."

She shook her head, and then she ran after them.

CHAPTER 5

The scene was absolute chaos.

There were reporters, police officers, firefighters, EMS teams, and bystanders all milling around the edges of the field, shouting and wailing and creating general confusion. The police were doing their best to hold the civilians back at a safe distance, but they had no idea what distance counted as "safe." They had set up a sort-of perimeter with their cars, but it was an incomplete barricade, to say the least, and there was so much noise in the melee that the officers were overwhelmed trying to keep the peace.

Because of all the hubbub, it was easy for Simon to slip through the perimeter.

"Simon!" Virgil shouted, watching him dodge between a pair of misaligned police cars near the thirty-yard line. He didn't hear a response, so he plowed through, too, blowing past the police officers and firefighters who were working hard to physically restrain a number of civilians.

They ran out onto the field. Simon skidded to a stop at the hash marks near the edge of the field, and Virgil ran up behind him, huffing and puffing and putting his hands on his knees. "What do we do?" Simon asked.

Still panting, Virgil looked up at the football players suspended above the ground by lightning bolts that were sticking out of their chests. "I don't know," he admitted.

"Llewyn should be here!" Simon cried with frustration.

But Virgil shook his head and put his hand on Simon's shoulder. "You know he can't be," he said. "It would kill him."

Simon sullenly shrugged his friend's hand off of his shoulder. "Yeah. I know."

The scene before them was exactly the same scene that they had seen on TV. That meant that the lightning tree, with all its murderous, electric branches, had been assaulting the players for at least half an hour now.

"Why isn't it leaving? What is it doing?" Simon asked desperately.

"I have no idea," Virgil admitted, "but I think it's safe to say that whatever it is, it is *not* lightning."

They looked around at the other people who were gathered around the field—the parents, the officers, the firemen, the bystanders—and there was one person who actually stood out against the entire crowd. It was a man who appeared to be in his mid-forties, who stood in the end zone, just a few feet away from the biggest group of levitating boys. The man was wearing the West Templar High School colors of blue and green, and he held a clipboard in his hand.

"Look at that," Abby said, coming up behind Simon and pointing at the man who appeared to be the coach. "He's standing five feet away from the players...why isn't he impaled by lightning, too?"

"No clue," Simon said, his attention clearly on the football players. His mind was racing with possible solutions, but as soon as the ideas came, they were struck back down. He couldn't seem to wrap his mind around a way to stop the lightning and free the players.

If they even *could* be freed.

Even if he found a way to stop the lightning, each of the bolts that ran the players through was at least a few inches in diameter. If the lightning stopped, the players would be left with gaping holes in their chests.

But *something* was keeping them alive, so whatever the lightning was, maybe it would leave them intact.

Maybe.

"We have to try," he murmured.

"What?" Virgil asked, but Simon wasn't paying attention. He had an idea.

He closed his eyes and clapped. An orange light burst out from his hands at the impact, and then faded…but Simon moved his lips, whispering the words Llewyn had taught them, and when he pulled his hands apart, the light between his palms formed a thick, round platter. Like the shield Virgil had summoned to drive the Brimstone Spire through the demon Asag's heart, the platter was inscribed with deep orange runes that glowed as if burning with their own fire. Simon gripped the platter like a Frisbee and took careful aim at the electrical pillar.

"That's not big enough to cut through the whole thing," Virgil pointed out.

"But maybe I can disrupt it," Simon replied. He drew in a deep breath and held it. Then he hurled the disc, throwing it as hard as he could toward the column of lightning.

It sailed toward the surging electric beam. Then, just before it struck, there was a low electrical rumble, a powering-down sound, and the lightning bolts drew themselves back to the beam, and the beam disappeared back up into the clouds, as if someone up in the sky had flipped a switch and cut the power. The football players fell back to the earth, their pads and helmets clattering, and the orange disc sailed through empty air, until it struck the announcer's booth on the far side of the field and blew a giant hole right through the center of it.

"You did it!" Virgil cried, incredulous.

But Simon shook his head. "No," he said, "I don't think I did."

There was a moment of stunned silence from the assembled crowd. Then everyone sprang into action. The first responders ran onto the field, splitting up without anyone having to give the order so that each fallen football player had at least one paramedic and one police officer by his side. "They're alive!" one of the officers shouted, sounding surprised. "Hey! Bring the stretchers—they're alive!" A team of paramedics popped open the doors of the ambulances in the parking lot and pulled out the wheeled stretchers. They rushed across the bumpy terrain and onto the football field, and together, the responders began loading up the gurneys and wheeling the players back to the ambulances.

Simon got a good look at one of the players as he was hurried by. The paramedics had pulled off his helmet, his jersey, and his shoulder pads so they could inspect his chest. Strangely, Simon saw, there was no hole in the boy's sternum like he had expected. There was just a circular burn mark, like a crusted-over smudge of cinders and ash. And he *was* alive, Simon could tell that easily, because his chest was rising and falling with labored breath.

He was alive, but he was changed.

His skin had shrunken and tightened, and his muscle and fat had been melted away, so he looked like a skeleton with just the barest covering of flesh. Most of the hair on his head had fallen out, and what was left was wispy and gray. The skin around his fingernails had pulled away, giving his nails an unnaturally long look. And he was gray and ashen all over, from his scalp down to his toes.

Simon took a step backward, startled at the sight of the teenage boy. Half an hour ago, he had been a strong, healthy athlete; now he was little more than a wasted, breathing mummy.

More gurneys rolled by, loaded with more players. Each and every one of them looked the same.

"What is this?" Simon asked, his blood chilling his veins like ice water. He felt something tug at his arm, and he looked down, feeling almost detached from his own body. It took him a second to register the fact that Virgil was pulling him away from the field.

"Come on. The cops are starting to give us weird looks," Virgil said, gently leading him away. "Let's go see Llewyn."

"Yeah," Abby agreed, taking Simon's other arm. Together, they walked back to the parking lot. "Llewyn will know what it is."

CHAPTER 6

Llewyn frowned. "I have no idea what it is."

The kinesthetic mage had met them at the opening to his tent. His long, blue wool coat flapped in the autumn wind that came whipping through the concrete drainage channel. He had his long, gray hair pulled back and tied with a thin leather strap, and his empty right eye socket glowed brilliant blue, even in the bright light of day. They had breathlessly explained what they had seen at West Templar High, and he had listened patiently, but with obvious growing concern.

"What do you mean you have no idea what it is? How is that possible?" Virgil cried. "You're a Kindle mage of the Order of the Phoenix!"

"I am a kinesthetic mage of the Seventh Order," Llewyn responded testily. "And what you describe is beyond the realm of my knowledge."

"Virgil brings up a decent point," Abby said gently. "Just how much of the magical world *exists* beyond the realm of your knowledge?"

Llewyn set his mouth into a hard line. He didn't much care for the questioning of his abilities. "I am one of the most powerful living sorcerers. My knowledge is vast. But magic is a deep well, as deep as the universe itself. Even the greatest mage has an understanding that amounts to a single planet in the gulf of infinite magic."

Virgil nudged Simon and whispered in his ear. "He's saying there's a lot he doesn't know."

Simon pushed Virgil off and tried to get them back on track. "It was awful, Llewyn. I'd never seen anything like it. Those football players are only a few years younger than we are, and they looked…I don't know….*shriveled*. Wasted away. But they were *alive*."

Llewyn nodded slowly. He pulled back the flap of the tent and ushered them inside. "Let's see what we can learn."

He led them into his vast mansion and down the infinite hallway. They passed through half a dozen doors, zig-zagging through the labyrinth of walls before they arrived at their destination: a dark, cavernous room with a massive white screen on the front wall and overstuffed chairs situated in a stadium style, facing the screen.

"Whoa! You have your own movie theatre?" Virgil said, bounding into the room and plopping down on one of the chairs. "Awesome!"

"It's not a theatre," the wizard corrected him. "It's a memory chamber."

Virgil shrugged. "Looks like a movie theatre," he insisted.

Llewyn motioned for Simon to follow him to the back of the room, where there stood something that looked like a stunted streetlamp in front of the wall. The base was greenish-gray iron, carved and sculpted with ornate scrollwork, and the lantern at the top was a small, empty clay dish protected by an octagonal glass box. The wizard held out one hand and said, "*Fís*," and a soft white flame sprang to life in the center of his palm. With his other hand, he opened the front pane of glass, and he placed the flame onto the clay dish inside. The fire slid off of his hand like a pat of butter and burned happily on the earthenware bowl, even though there was no fuel to feed it or keep it alive. Then the wizard closed the pane of glass, and he lifted up his other hand. The iron pillar beneath the lantern rose with it, growing taller and taller until Llewyn closed his hand into a fist. The streetlamp came to a rest just at Simon's eye level.

"Stand here," Llewyn instructed, moving Simon so that he stood directly in front of the lamp, with his back turned to the light and his eyes facing the movie screen.

"Okay," Simon said nervously, trying not to fidget. "What… am I doing?"

Llewyn grunted. "You're going to show me your memory."

He said a quick spell, and Simon's spine stiffened. He felt the inside of his head fill with warmth, as if someone had turned on a space heater in his skull. The flame in the lantern behind him flared brighter, and its light shot into the back of Simon's head and came out through his forehead, and then Simon understood.

The flame was the projector light; his brain was the filmstrip.

"Whoa!" Virgil shouted, sitting up straight in his seat. The image that the flame was projecting on the movie screen was a direct copy of what Simon was seeing through his own eyes. At that moment, the screen showed the backs of the chairs, the back of Virgil's head, and the movie screen in the background.

The background movie screen had the same projection, except smaller, and the background movie screen in *that* smaller projection had its own even *smaller* projection, and on and on until the image got so small, it became just a speck.

The whole thing made Simon feel motion-sick.

"Now, close your eyes and try to remember what you saw," Llewyn instructed. "If I see the particulars, I might be able to piece together an idea of what we may be dealing with."

Simon closed his eyes, and the image on the screen went dark. He pictured the football field in his mind, and the same vision of it faded into view at the front of the room.

"Wow," Virgil said, sounding impressed. "We can *actually* see what he's thinking."

The knowledge that three other people in the room were watching his thoughts made Simon feel self-conscious, and incredibly nervous. His face grew hot, and the tips of his ears burned red. What if he accidentally conjured up the wrong image? Memory was funny like that…one second, you're remembering a sorcery-crime on a high school football field, the next second, you're thinking about the girl you have a crush on, and then—

"Ah-ha-ha!" Virgil burst out laughing. "It's Abby! Aww, Simon's thinking of Abby!"

"I am not!" Simon hollered, trying to push the image of Abby from his mind. But the more he tried to ignore it, the more solid the image of her became. Specifically, it was the image of her touching his arm that first day they had met a couple of months before, when she had felt his sadness.

Abby quietly cleared her throat, and Simon couldn't tell if it was an embarrassed sound, or a sweet one, or an angry one. Probably an angry one. He couldn't bear to open his eyes, to face her right now. Virgil was laughing his head off, and Llewyn was grunting with audible annoyance. He could only imagine how Abby might be feeling, but he couldn't push the image of her away.

So he did something drastic.

He took the hand that was away from everyone else, out of their view, and placed the palm against the side of his leg. He pushed his magic into the hand, and it warmed against his jeans. Then he bit down hard and forced a jolt of electricity down his arm, and it popped out of his hand, shocking his leg. He whimpered with the pain of it, and his mind went red in reaction to the pain. The image of Abby was wiped off of the movie screen, and the electrical shock reminded Simon of the lightning column on the football field, so the image that was projected at the front of the room when the red mask melted away was once again the scene at the high school.

"Aw…no fun," Virgil complained. He sank back down in his seat and crossed his arms.

"Good," Llewyn muttered. He walked around the chairs and moved closer to the front of the room to get a better look at the image on the screen. "Walk me through it."

In his memory, Simon saw the great column of energy and light, crackling with power and fury. He saw the individual bolts of lightning sticking out like tree branches, with the twitching, screaming football players skewered through their chests. He saw the confused and helpless looks of the first responders.

"What happened next?" Llewyn asked.

Simon pressed the play button in his mind. The scene rolled forward; Virgil, Abby, and Llewyn watched from Simon's point of view as he formed the magical disc with the dark runes and hurled it toward the energy column. Then they saw the column and its branches fizzle out of existence, and they saw the purple-gold clouds in the sky close up, as if sealing off the power. The football players dropped to the ground like dead flies, and the paramedics rushed in.

The fifty-yard line was marked with a huge, charred circle of scorched earth.

"Show me the players," Llewyn said, directing the memory movie. Simon flashed to the close-up memory of the first football player who had rolled by him on the gurney, with his withered skin and wispy hair.

Llewyn studied the picture for a good three minutes, his alert green eye seeing much that the boys couldn't see, or didn't know how to see. Finally, he said, "Is there anything else?"

"No," Simon replied, opening his eyes. The memory image on the movie screen was replaced by his real-time vision again. "After that, we got into the cars and came straight here."

"Any idea what it might be?" Virgil asked.

The sorcerer was lost in thought. "Not exactly," he admitted. He whispered the word *"Dorcha,"* and the flame in the clay dish inside the lantern extinguished itself. Simon felt the magic leave his head, and the screen at the front of the room went mercifully dark.

"It's some sort of intense-heat withering," Llewyn continued, after finding the right word. "A slow frying of the body. I've seen version of it before, but never like this. Not on this scale. Not with an entire football team's worth of victims at once." His face darkened, and the blue light in his right eye socket turned to a gemstone purple. "Never with children," he said, his voice uneven with anger.

"Who would want to do that?" Abby asked uneasily. She had felt sadness and anger and spite and fury and jealousy and greed and a thousand other negative energies from powerful and petty people and monsters. But she had never felt a rage so strong that it would sap the lives of thirty high schoolers at once, and with such prolonged, sustained agony.

"I don't even know who would have the *power* to do that," Llewyn countered. His hand moved absently to his chest, touching the black shard lodged in his sternum beneath his shirt and coat. "Even at my full power, I couldn't sustain a column of energy that powerful for more than ten or fifteen seconds. You say this one was live for half an hour?"

"At least," Virgil said. "We got there about fifteen minutes after we saw it on the news, and it had to have been there long enough for people to notice it and for the news to hear about it and send out a crew to go live with it."

Llewyn considered this. Then he shook his head. "Impossible."

But it wasn't impossible. It had happened, and by now, all of Templar had seen it. All of the *world* had probably seen it; the news footage was undoubtedly making the rounds on social media.

Virgil pulled out his phone and typed "Templar Pennsylvania" into YouTube. "Yep," he said, holding up the phone so everyone could see the footage. "Fifteen thousand likes and counting."

"It's on YouTube?!" Simon said. "Why didn't we watch the video instead of combing through my brain with a magic light?!" He still hadn't even attempted to make eye contact with Abby out of embarrassment.

"Because I don't know what YouTube is," Llewyn said, annoyed. He snatched Virgil's phone and glared at the screen. "Impossible," he murmured again. He peered closely at the newsreel video. "Wait. Stop it. How do I stop it?" he asked, shaking the phone. "Rewind!" he commanded it.

"Whoa, whoa, whoa! Easy!" Virgil said. He reached out and took the phone out of Llewyn's hands.

"Rewind it," the old magician commanded.

"I'm rewinding it, I'm rewinding it!" He scrubbed the video backward a few seconds, then held out the screen so Llewyn could see it. "Look, but don't touch," he said.

Llewyn watched the footage carefully. "Stop!" he bellowed. Virgil paused the video. The sorcerer peered closely and asked, "Can you make it larger?"

Virgil pinched his fingers out on the screen and zoomed in. "What am I looking for?"

"That," Llewyn said, stubbing his finger against the image.

Simon and Abby came up closer, and all four of them looked down at Virgil's phone. The frame was a close-up shot of the football field and the lightning tree. On the far side of the field stood the metal bleachers that flanked the announcer's box, and behind the bleachers were dark woods. Llewyn was pointing to the spot where the bleachers ended, near the end of the field.

There was a person standing there, a woman dressed in a long, purple cloak, with a deep purple hood that was pulled up over her head, hiding her features from view. She wore a pair of long, gold gloves, and her hands were clasped together at her waist. She seemed to be simply standing there, observing the fracas and going unseen as little more than a piece of background scenery.

Virgil hit play, and the video advanced. All four of them kept their eyes glued to the figure at the end of the stands. She continued to watch the madness, right up until the lightning tree fizzled out of existence. Once it had vanished, the woman inclined her head, turned her back on the field, and disappeared into the woods.

"She's the culprit," Llewyn said, straightening up and walking out of the room. "We need to find her. Soon. Before she strikes again."

CHAPTER 7

"How exactly *do* we find her?"

They were winding their way back through the maze of hallways, Llewyn leading the way, his footsteps falling heavily with determination.

"We'll try the Font of Finding," the wizard said.

He led them back out to the main hallway, then he turned and strode up to the circular door at the end of the hall, the same door he had taken Simon and Virgil through on their very first visit to his magical tent. He pulled open the door and motioned them inside.

"I've got to get to work," Abby said apologetically. "But let me know if I can help." Llewyn nodded at her, and she turned to go. But before she did, she reached out and touched Simon's sleeve. "Come find me later?" she asked, her voice lilting with hopefulness.

Simon blushed, but he nodded. "Definitely," he said.

Abby smiled, and her eyes brightened behind her glasses. "Good." Then she hurried down the hallway and back out the door, into the outside world.

"Come on," Llewyn gruffed. Simon and Virgil hopped through the doorway, and the wizard stepped in behind them, closing the door and sealing them all inside.

They walked the pier-like platform over to the stone basin, where Llewyn formed his brilliant orange globe and set it into the stone. As they watched, the orange coloring swirled away from the surface, replaced by the familiar asphalt gray, and the orange bits collected into the energy signatures of magical beings in Templar, and beyond.

Llewyn frowned as he studied the globe. He moved his hands over the surface, and sometimes he would poke and prod at an orange dot, inspecting it carefully. He was unsatisfied each time. Soon he had examined every square inch of the gray-and-orange ball. "I can't see her," he said, furrowing his brow.

"What does that means? She doesn't have a magic signature? She doesn't have any powers?" Simon asked, confused.

Llewyn scratched his cheek. "That is one possible explanation. But not a likely one. Someone utilized an extraordinary amount of magic to make the lightning column. An energy signature like that should show itself clearly. *Very* clearly." He waved his hands, and the globe broke into small pieces of ash and flaked away, dissolving completely in the air. "The more likely explanation is that her power is cloaked."

Simon considered this. "What would it take for someone to hide magic from a wizard at your power level?" he asked.

The wizard gritted his teeth. "It would take a lot."

"Okay, so what do we do?" Virgil asked.

Llewyn's face darkened. "We either track her down, or we wait for her to strike again."

"If she strikes again, won't more people get hurt?" Virgil asked. Llewyn and Simon both gave him a look. "Oh," he said, blushing. "Right. You meant that as a not-actual choice."

Llewyn led them out of the chamber and back toward the front of the tent. "Go back to the high school and see if she left any trail," he instructed. He stopped at the chest in the sitting room and pulled it open. He reached in and grabbed a small packet of seeds. "If you find one of her footprints, plant one of these seeds there. It will help you track her down."

"What is it?" Simon asked, looking curiously at them. Each one was about the size of a watermelon seed, but emerald green in color, with thin blue veins stretching across the surface.

"Ripple ferns," he said, as if this simple phrase explained everything. He ushered them out. "Move now," he urged them, holding open the door. "Look carefully, and work quickly. If we don't find this woman soon, people may start dying."

CHAPTER 8

"I always wanted to be a Hardy Boy," Virgil said, rolling his eyes.

"Hey, the Hardy Boys were awesome," Simon said defensively.

Virgil pressed his lips together thoughtfully. "Yeah…I guess that's true," he admitted.

They were back at West Templar High, standing at the edge of the bleachers, right around the spot where they had seen the woman in the purple cloak stand in the video. The football field itself was cordoned off with police tape now, and there were a couple of officers lingering over the burn mark at center field. They gave Simon and Virgil suspicious looks when they approached the field, but the boys had given them an awkward wave, and since they skirted around the police tape instead of approaching the field, the officers let them go. Every few minutes, though, one of them would look over at the bleachers and scowl.

Virgil pulled out his phone and brought up the video on YouTube. He zoomed in on the woman in the cloak and held up the phone, using the image to verify his own position. "Yeah, looks like she was about here," he decided. He put the phone to sleep and slipped it into his pocket. "See anything weird?"

"I don't see any footprints," Simon said, crouching down and scanning the grass.

"Neither do I," Virgil confirmed. "Should we plant one of the seeds anyway? See what happens?"

"Yeah, 'cause the one thing I really want to do with something that possesses a magical power that I don't understand is use it in a way that was *not* included in the instructions," Simon said.

Virgil pouted. "You're no fun."

Simon mumbled his agreement, and he continued to search the ground. "Hey, how's your shoulder?" he asked, nodding up toward the arm Virgil had broken during their fight with Asag.

"Better!" Virgil said, flexing his fingers and spinning his arm like a windmill. "I thought it would still be sore after the cast came off last week, but it feels totally normal. Except for when it rains. It gets a little stiff when it rains. When I woke up on Tuesday, I couldn't really move it for half an hour or so, 'cause of the storm. Aside from that, it's pretty good."

"Small price to pay for saving the world from a demon from the eighth circle of hell," Simon said with a wry grin.

"Easy for you to say," Virgil replied.

They continued to search the area, making small circles between the bleachers and the field, looking for any print the woman might have left.

"I've got nothing," Virgil said after several more minutes of searching.

"The ground's too dry," Simon agreed. "We haven't had any rain since that storm on Monday, we need the ground to be wetter and—" Simon stopped short. The wheels in his brain were turning smoothly, and an idea was forming in his head.

"What?" Virgil asked.

Simon looked up at him, his eyes brightening. "The creek," he said, pointing to the trees behind the bleachers. "The creek in the woods!"

"What about it?"

"It rained on Monday, and the creek down there gets filled with overflow when the river gets too high."

"So?"

Simon made an exasperated look with his eyes. "*So*, we had a big storm on Monday, and if it rained enough to raise the river, it would have flooded the creek, so the creek bank would have been higher, and by now it must have receded, and that means the banks are now...?" He trailed off his question, twirling his hands in the air and waiting for Virgil to finish his thought.

Virgil blinked. "The banks are now...banking?"

Simon slapped his forehead with his palm. "Virgil! The banks are wet! The banks are muddy! The banks were under water, but now they're not, and the ground right here is too dry for her to leave footprints, but she went back into the woods, toward the creek, and the ground down *there* is wet enough and soft enough from the flooding for her to have left a footprint!"

Virgil nodded slowly as the pieces fell into place. "Wow, you really *are* a Hardy Boy," he said.

"Thanks," Simon said smugly.

Virgil snorted. "That wasn't a compliment. I've reconsidered my stance...the Hardy Boys were total nerds."

They walked across the narrow strip of grass that connected the football field to the woods, moving slowly and keeping their heads down, looking for any sign of the woman's tracks. When they approached the edge of the woods, they stopped and peered into the thicket of trees. Even though it was the afternoon, and the sun was still bright and fairly high in the sky, the woods seemed darker, and ominous somehow. Most of the trees still had their leaves, though they had been drained of their brilliant autumn colors and had faded to a desaturated and mottled brown. The leaves not only blocked out the direct sunlight, but also seemed to swallow up the diffuse brightness of the world.

"Do woods always look so creepy?" Virgil asked, fighting off a chill.

Simon nodded. "Yeah. Pretty much always."

"Okay, then."

There was a small trail that wound into the woods on their right, a narrow footpath that had been made by several decades' worth of children stomping and crashing their way through the underbrush. "She probably used the trail," Virgil said, indicating the path. "Not as many branches or brush there to snag on her cloak."

Simon raised an eyebrow, a little impressed in spite of himself. "Nice deduction, Nancy Drew."

They stepped onto the path and entered the dark, foreboding woods.

The sunlight wasn't the only thing the trees swallowed up; they also absorbed the sounds of the city, so that even after just a few feet, Simon and Virgil could no longer hear the sound of traffic on the road outside the high school, and the dull chatter of the two police officers on the football field fell away. All they could hear was the crunching of the leaves underneath their own feet.

The woods were deeper than they appeared from the outside, and soon they could no longer see the edge of the school property when they turned back to look. "Were there always so many trees here?" Virgil asked.

Simon shrugged. "Guess so. They probably wanted a big enough barrier between the school and the interstate to keep out the sounds of the traffic."

"Well, couldn't we have built a sound wall like a normal city?" Virgil asked. He couldn't quite keep that chill from prickling through his shoulders.

After a few more minutes, the trail led them to the creek. It was running hard, with little eddies swirling up in the water as it rushed down the rocks, but it wasn't particularly high. Whatever flooding had occurred earlier in the week had long since washed downstream, and the creek had leveled out.

"Look," Simon said, pointing down into the mud. "Bingo."

There were three footprints in the soft earth, prints made by a woman's shoes, from the look of it; they could make out the impression of a narrow heel, and the print was much smaller than either of their own shoes. The prints led down to the water's edge. Simon peered across the stream; there were two more prints leading away from the creek. The first one on the far side was deeper than any of the other prints. "She must have hopped over," he surmised.

"All joking aside, we're pretty good at being detectives," Virgil said, clearly impressed by their uncanny abilities. "We should open our own detective agency."

"We just *did* open our own detective agency."

"We opened a laundromat."

"Oh, give it a rest." Simon fished the packet of seeds out of his pocket. He tore open the package and plucked one of the green and blue seeds from inside. "Where do you think you buy something like this?" he asked, examining it carefully.

"That's a good question," Virgil admitted. "Like, where did Llewyn get *any* of that stuff in his chest?" He had been referring to the large trunk in the sitting room, but the way he worded it put both of them in mind of the gleaming black blade that was ever-burrowing into Llewyn's chest, toward his heart.

Without saying a word, they agreed to let the question drop.

Simon took the seed between his fingers and pushed it down into the wet soil, directly in the center of the woman's footprint. He sank it about an inch into the dirt, then he covered it with loose topsoil.

Then they waited.

"Is that it?" Virgil whispered, speaking softly, as if he were afraid he might disturb the seed.

"I don't know," Simon replied.

"Should we water it?"

"I don't know," Simon said again, sounding annoyed this time.

"It's just, usually you water seeds if you want them to grow," Virgil pointed out.

"Virgil! I don't know!" Simon hissed. "Why don't you go get some water from the creek and water the stupid seed, if you're so worried about it."

Virgil glanced down at the rushing water. It looked cold. "Nah," he decided. "I'm sure it'll be fine."

The seed proved him right. As they looked on, a tiny sprout pushed its way through the earth, curling like a tendril. It grew quickly, yawning up toward the canopy of the trees, and soon it was joined by another sprout, and then another, and then another. After just a few seconds, the entire footprint was filled with small green shoots, all curling and writhing and growing straight upward.

Simon pulled Virgil back from the footprint as they watched, mesmerized. The shoots began to twist together, forming two separate, thick stalks, each one made up of dozens of growing green tendrils. The stalks grew taller and thicker as the sprouts filled out and increased in size. Soon, each of the stalks was as big around as a human leg. They were so big that the footprint could no longer contain them, and they separated from each other, one pushing out to the left, one pushing out to the right, dragging a narrow channel in the soil between them. It was like the footprint itself had split in two and burst out sideways from its mooring in the mud.

The stalks continued to grow. After a few feet, they spread out near the top, the thick tendrils reaching from one stalk to the other, and they became connected, like a high bridge. Then, as one solid trunk, they began to grow straight up again, until Simon finally understood what they were seeing.

"It's building a person!" he said, his voice tight with the thrill of a new magic.

"I think it's building the person who belongs to the footprint," Virgil said.

They watched as the ripple fern wove together its shoots and stalks, forming the shape of a woman, fingers and eyelashes and ears and all. It was like watching an invisible artist form a remarkably lifelike human sculpture in fast-forward. When the last stalk closed up over the figure's skull, completing the sculpture, the stalks began to pop with tiny buds. After just a few seconds, the buds coated the woman-sculpture like chicken pox, and then, all at once, they burst open, exploding in a massive puff of fern leaves. It happened so suddenly that Simon and Virgil both jumped in surprise, and when they settled back down, they stared at the sculpture in amazement; the fern leaves had sprouted and spread in the perfect shape of the woman's cloak, including the hood that she had pulled down over her head.

"It's her," Virgil murmured in awe. He circled the sculpture, inspecting it from a safe distance. "It's her *exactly*."

"Incredible," Simon whispered.

The fern leaves waved in the breeze, in the exact same way that a full cloak would move. But then Virgil realized that there *was* no breeze, and that the fern-cloak was moving on its own. "What's it doing?" he asked, alarmed.

Simon's eyes grew wide with amazement. "It's *remembering*."

As they watched, the leaves began to rustle faster and faster, and soon the motion effect was completely seamless.

Then the ripple fern raised one foot and took a step forward.

Virgil nearly jumped out of his skin, and he shrieked with surprise. But the fern-statue didn't seem to hear. She took a second step forward, grabbed the bottom half of her cloak, hiked it up over her ankles, and leapt across the creek.

"I get it!" Simon said aloud, though perhaps not fully aware that he was actually speaking what he was thinking. "The ripple fern shows what happened. It's like watching a recreation of the woman from that day."

"No kidding," Virgil muttered. He was already a few steps ahead of Simon on that one. "So what do we do?" he asked, watching the ripple fern step quickly up the far side of the creek bed.

"We follow her," Simon replied.

They jumped across the creek, slipping a little in the soft earth, and hustled after the fern. It moved quickly, for a plant, and as they found themselves winding through the trees, Simon started to breathe heavily. "We should do more cardio," he suggested.

"Speak for yourself," Virgil replied, also breathing hard. "I'm in great shape."

After a few hundred feet, the ripple fern stopped, walking briskly up to a big, moss-covered boulder sticking up out of the dirt. Simon and Virgil watched from a safe distance, even though Simon was fairly certain that the fern-statue couldn't actually see them, but could only go through the same motions that its original source-woman had.

Still, he figured...better safe than sorry.

The ripple fern put her hands on the stone and gave it a mighty push. It tilted back easily, like it was on hinges. And upon closer inspection, Virgil and Simon found that it *was* on hinges—two rusty hinges secured the base of the boulder to a hidden metal chute that was buried beneath the ground, and that fact now became visible as the rock tilted backward, revealing the open space beneath. The metal chute sank down into the earth, further down than they could see from their vantage points. There was a ladder fastened to the chute that led down into the darkness, and the ripple fern slipped down onto the ladder and disappeared into the underground chute, closing the boulder behind her.

Virgil blinked at Simon. "Don't tell me you want to go down *there*," he said.

Simon frowned. He very much did *not* want to go down there. "This might be our only chance of finding her before she strikes again," he groaned. "I think we *have* to go down there."

Virgil sighed. "Being the heroes of Templar sucks."

They pushed back the boulder and gazed down the square hole into the darkness below. Simon pulled out his phone, clicked on the flashlight, and aimed it into the void.

The light didn't even come close to finding the bottom.

"Paper-rock-scissors to see who goes first?" Simon suggested.

Virgil nodded. It was standard operating procedure.

It only took two throws for Simon to win the best of three.

"Aw, come on," Virgil whined. "You cheated."

"Maybe you should try throwing something besides scissors every single time," Simon countered.

Virgil snorted. "I don't throw scissors every single time," he muttered. But rules were rules; Virgil clicked on the flashlight on his own phone, held it carefully in one hand, and lowered himself onto the ladder, moving slowly downward into the darkness.

If the woods themselves were quiet, then the vertical tunnel beneath the ground was as silent as a tomb. All Virgil could hear was the ringing of his own ears and the scuffling sounds of his feet dragging across the metal rungs of the ladder as he descended. He kept looking down, trying to see what was waiting for him in the murky darkness below, but because of his grip on the rungs as he climbed down, the flashlight on his phone was of very little help; the beam kept veering in this direction and that direction, depending on his grip, and it almost never pointed straight down.

So he descended into darkness, praying he would hit the bottom soon, and that the ripple fern wouldn't be waiting for him when he got there. Everything he understood about the fern—which was very, very little—pointed to the idea that the plant sculpture couldn't react to his presence, but a semi-sentient magical fern wasn't exactly the kind of thing you could hold to normal rules of logic and expectation.

Then he took one more step down, and his foot came to a rest on soft, solid earth. Virgil exhaled with relief. "Found the bottom," he called up to Simon, who was about halfway down the ladder. Simon had left the boulder tilted backward, and a bit of sunlight filtered down through the opening to the hole. It looked so far away, not much bigger than a nickel from Virgil's perspective. "We might be deeper than the subway," he said.

As Simon continued his careful climb down the ladder, Virgil shone his phone flashlight in a circle, inspecting their new situation. The ladder had led him down to a small clearing under the earth, with a long tunnel breaking out in one direction. If his bearings were right, the tunnel headed east, toward the Appalachians.

Simon made his way to the bottom of the ladder and joined Virgil on the ground. He wiped his hands on his jeans and reached for his own light, shining it down the tunnel. "I don't see the fern," he said, squinting down the earthen hallway. "Did you lose her?"

"Well, I would say maybe *we* lost her," Virgil said pointedly. "The woman in the cloak must have been moving a lot more quickly than two guys who have no idea what this tunnel is, or where it goes, or why it's here, or what's waiting for them down in the darkness."

"Fair point," Simon admitted.

Virgil frowned as he peered down the empty tunnel. "So what do we do?"

"You always ask that like you don't already know the answer," Simon replied.

Virgil sighed. "Yeah. I know."

Then, in unison, they said, "We go after her."

"I went first down the ladder," Virgil pointed out. "It's your turn to go first."

Simon frowned. He couldn't think of a single thing he wanted to do less than walk down that tunnel. But fair was fair. He held up the light in front of him, and he began to creep down the hall.

They moved in silence, each of them feeling the skin on their shoulders prickling with fear of the darkness, and of the unknown. Simon had a pretty good handle on the history and workings of Templar, but he had never even heard so much as a rumor about underground walkways connecting different parts of the city. Yet the tunnel didn't seem newly-constructed; the dirt wasn't freshly wet, but crusted over with mineral deposits, as if it had been dug out many years before. But it only went in one direction, and as far as the flashlight could uncover, there were no branches in the tunnel, so if they followed it to its terminus, even if they didn't catch up to the ripple fern, they would still find the place where the woman in the purple cloak had surfaced. And that would be an important piece of the puzzle. He opened his mouth to say as much to Virgil, just for the sake of breaking the silence, when suddenly he saw a flash of brilliant white flash at the far end of the tunnel.

It surged toward them, as fast as a bolt of lightning.

"Stop!" Simon screamed. Instinctively, he dropped his

phone and threw up his hands, conjuring two heavy shields. They exploded into being in the nick of time; no sooner had they formed than a heavy bolt of lightning cracked against them, driving Simon backward, his feet dragging through the hardened dirt.

The bolt of lightning didn't evaporate like a normal lightning bolt. It held steady, fizzling against Simon's shields with electric fury. The power surge was constant, and as hard as Simon pushed back with his kinesthetic shields, the lightning pushed harder, and it dragged him backward through the tunnel.

"It's a trap!" Virgil cried. He stumbled backward, his eyes wide with horror as he tried to stay ahead of Simon's retreat. He tripped over a clump of hard earth and fell onto his seat, then crab-walked back toward the ladder, his heart racing. "Simon!" he screamed, his throat tight with helplessness.

Simon didn't reply. Simon *couldn't* reply. He was using all his energy and all of his strength to hold the lightning bolt at bay. It was obvious now that the jagged line of pulsing light and power was the same type of lightning bolt that had shot out of the energy column on the West Templar High football field and had impaled the members of the football team. If it broke through his shield, it would impale him, too, and he would be fried from the inside, dried up, with nothing left of him but a skeleton wrapped in pinched, papery skin.

Beads of sweat formed on Simon's forehead and spilled down his brow as he gritted his teeth and pushed back against the lightning bolt. It surged forward, crackling with power, and Simon's outer shield began to split. The energy was flaking away pieces of the solid orange surface, and the entire kinesthetic plate began to break, the interior splintering like ice cracking under a weight. "I can't hold it!" Simon screamed.

"Fifty more feet!" Virgil screamed back. In truth, he had no idea how many more feet Simon had to go before he reached the ladder back up to the surface. He was terrible with numbers. But it seemed both believable and achievable, and so he ran with it, pushing himself back to his feet and running toward the end of the tunnel.

Simon tried to say that he didn't have fifty feet worth of strength left in him, but only got as far as "I don't have—" before the bolt cracked completely through the first shield. The orange shards of the kinesthetic barrier fell away, and Simon threw up his other hand, taking the brunt of the lightning bolt with his new shield. The surface of that one instantly started flaking away. "Virgil!" Simon cried, directing his voice backwards over his shoulder. "Refraction!"

Virgil turned pale. *Refraction* was a new spell that Llewyn was teaching them, and it was complex. They'd dedicated three whole days to it over the course of the last two weeks, and neither Simon nor Virgil had gotten it right. One time, during an attempt that went extremely wrong, Virgil had actually managed to split Simon into three separate pieces. Thankfully, a by-product of the spell was a serious numbing component; Simon didn't feel anything, and Llewyn had pressed him back together in half of a flash, so there was no lasting harm done.

But still. Refraction was very much a work in progress.

"It's not ready!" Virgil hollered back.

But Simon was insistent. "Refraction!" he screamed again. His new shield was splintering, and he couldn't form enough magic in his spent left hand to conjure up another one. It was clear that his only chance of survival was to get back to the ladder, and he was alternating backward steps with the skidding of his sneakers against the dirt from the force of the lightning bolt, but it was slow going. He couldn't run backward; he wasn't great with balance to begin with, and the added push of the lightning would knock him off-kilter, and he would trip, there was no question about it. He would hit the ground, and then the lightning would hit Virgil, and even if it didn't, it would fill the tunnel, and their chances of escaping without being burned up by its energy were low. Besides, the thing seemed to have some sort of built-in homing system; anytime Simon scooted a little to the left or a little to the right, the bolt moved with him, keeping his chest directly in its sights.

Odds were that even if he fell, the mystical bolt would follow him to the ground, and he wouldn't make it out of the tunnel alive.

"Refraction!" he cried. "*Now!*"

Virgil gritted his teeth in panic. It was highly likely he would split Simon into pieces again, or maybe something worse. Something that would kill them both. But if he *didn't* refract the lightning bolt, it would break through Simon's shield. There wasn't enough room in the tunnel for Virgil to scoot by, throw up his own shield, and take the attack head-on, and at the rate the thing had cut through Simon's first shield, it still wouldn't give them enough time to reach the ladder.

Simon was right. Refraction was their only hope.

"Okay!" he screamed back, wringing his hands with hopelessness. "Okay! Refraction!" He shook out his fingers, which suddenly felt stiff and frozen, now that they were being called upon. "I don't—" he started, but that wasn't quite right. He tried again: "I can't—" But that wasn't right either. A lump formed in his throat as he said, "Simon, I'm sorry if this goes wrong."

Simon didn't reply. He was too focused on holding the strength of his last shield, which was shot through with cracks and ready to collapse at any second. But he nodded, almost imperceptibly. Virgil saw it, and it gave him a small surge of strength.

It wasn't a big surge. But he would take what he could get.

He closed his eyes and put the heels of his hands together, forming a butterfly with his palms and fingers, just as Llewyn had shown them. Most of the spells they had learned so far relied on them drawing from the strength they carried within themselves, but the refraction spell was different. It relied on external energy. "Yin and Yang," Llewyn had explained during one of their sessions. "A true sorcerer doesn't rely on just one source of power. Your inner energy will deplete as you use it. Magic that draws from outside the self will give your body a chance to replenish its internal energy."

Virgil was grateful for that now. He could have drawn a decent amount of energy from his gut, certainly. But with that magical lightning bolt crackling through the tunnel, he had a hunch that the energy he could draw from the exterior world was pretty substantial at that particular moment.

Keeping the heels of his hands pressed firmly together, he pulled back against the strength in the air, dragging out energy like water drops from a rain cloud. Tiny flecks of light shot through the air, most of them flowing down from the lightning bolt, and they collected in the hollow space between his palms. Soon he had collected a bundle of crackling blue energy about the size of a tennis ball within his hands. He held it there, cradled between his palms, fusing the particles of energy together with his will, and he opened his eyes.

Simon's splintering shield was a product of his right hand, and with his empty left hand, he had gripped his right wrist, giving the shield extra stabilization. But the shield was almost all the way cracked through, and Simon had just seconds before the bolt shattered the kinesthetic magic and shot through his chest.

"Virgil!" Simon screamed again.

A sudden calm fell over Virgil like a blanket. It was the

relaxation of shock, with its apathetic detachment and cool calculation. He dropped to one knee, to give himself a sturdier base for the spell. He held out his hands, still joined at the heels, and positioned them directly in front of his chest, where his heart-center could funnel its power most easily through his arms and into the gathered energy. The words of Llewyn's spell rang clearly between his ears, more clearly than they had the many, many times that Llewyn had actually said them in their presence. "*Caelum protero, aeris vorso, aeris verso*," he breathed, feeling the words collect their own special power as they formed on his tongue and escaped his lips. The blue ball of energy began to spin. It turned faster and faster, until its edges became a soft blur of motion. Then, suddenly, it sucked in on itself and disappeared completely with a soft *pop*.

"Now!" Virgil yelled.

Simon dove to the ground, and just as he did, a clear, glass-like wall crystallized in the air between the two men and the lightning bolt. The energy hit the wall, and the wall absorbed its power, then turned it backward and shot it back down the tunnel, refracting the energy in half a dozen different directions. The lightning bolt had become six lightning bolts, zig-zagging along the tunnel and shooting back toward its source.

The refraction spell had worked.

"Nice work," Simon said, breathing a sigh of relief.

"Congratulate me later," Virgil said, jumping to his feet and pulling Simon up behind him. "I don't know how long it'll hold."

They ran to the ladder. They could hear the refraction wall starting to crack behind them. Simon grabbed ahold of the ladder and began pulling himself up. Virgil glanced uneasily at the refraction; the lightning bolt was breaking through. "Faster would be good," he warned.

"I'm going!" Simon hollered back. His foot slipped, and he fell down a rung, smacking his elbow on one of the flat metal bars. "Ow!"

"Simon! Move!"

Simon found his footing and pushed himself upward. Virgil leapt up behind him, grabbing a rung that was about three feet higher than his head. He clutched it and held on tightly, dangling for a second over the floor of the tunnel as the lightning bolt broke through the refraction and slammed against the back wall of the tunnel, just beneath Virgil's feet.

He planted his feet on the ladder and scrambled up the chute behind Simon, out of the tunnel and back into the dismal woods.

CHAPTER 9

"Well. We lost her," Virgil said.

"Your ability to state the obvious never ceases to amaze," Simon said dryly.

They were back in the Pontiac, driving down the interstate back toward their apartment. "Do you think Llewyn's going to be mad?" Virgil asked.

Simon snorted. "I don't think he's going to love it," he said.

Virgil thought about the ripple fern and the lightning in the tunnel as the white lines flashed by on the road outside the car. "Maybe he'll be so grateful that we didn't die, he'll forget to be mad."

"I think it's possible to be both glad that we're alive and mad that we lost our only lead at the same time."

"Yeah. That's true." Virgil sighed. He pressed his head against the passenger window. The glass felt cool against his skin. "I wish he didn't have that black magic in his chest. Just seeing what he can do with half his magic tied behind his back…can you imagine what he'd be able to do at full power?"

Simon nodded. "It sure would make our lives a whole lot easier."

"He'd have shut that lightning bolt down."

"Yep," Simon nodded.

Virgil cleared his throat. "I guess what I'm saying is, it's his fault we lost the ripple fern, really, and we should be clear about that when we tell him."

"Oh, yeah," Simon nodded, feigning enthusiasm. "That's a bang-up idea."

"Good. I'm glad we agree," Virgil said, satisfied.

Simon sighed.

They drove the rest of the way to the apartment in silence, each of them thinking his own thoughts and processing the extraordinary events of the day. When they finally pulled up outside their building, Simon threw the car into park, but he didn't shut off the engine.

"You coming?" Virgil asked, unbuckling his seat belt.

Simon smiled bashfully. "No," he said.

Virgil raised an eyebrow. "No?"

"Nope."

"But you live here."

"I know that," Simon replied.

"So why aren't you coming inside?"

The tips of Simon's ears burned pink. "Because Abby's shift is almost over," he said.

Virgil's face lit up with understanding. "Oh ho ho ho!" he cried, clapping his hands together excitedly. "Oh ho *ho!* I *see!*"

"Virgil…" Simon began, rolling his eyes.

But Virgil held up a hand, silencing him. "Say no more!" he said, popping open his door. "I heard what she said. 'Simon, come find me after my shift! I need you! I *want* you!'"

"She didn't say that," Simon pointed out.

"Never let it be said that Virgil Matter got between his best friend and a date!"

"It's not a date," Simon said.

"Oh! Take her to Lookout Point!" Virgil gasped.

"I'm not taking her to Lookout P—"

"Take her to Lookout Point, and tell her you wanted to give her the best view of Templar, because she's new to town and probably hasn't seen the whole city yet!" Virgil shook his head slowly, in total awe of his own brilliance. "I should go on more dates. I am so good at planning them."

"Will you get out?" Simon asked, his patience starting to wear thin. He glanced at the clock; Abby's shift at Squeezy Cheez would be over in ten minutes.

"*You* get out," Virgil grinned, stepping out of the car.

"That doesn't make any sense," Simon pointed out.

Virgil stood on the curb, and his grin grew so wide, his teeth looked like they might fall out. "I won't wait up," he said with a wink.

"Go," Simon instructed.

Virgil hovered in the doorway a few seconds longer, smiling that smile, then he stood up and closed the door. Simon threw the car into drive and pulled away from the curb. He saw Virgil waving wildly in his rearview mirror.

Simon took some deep breaths as he maneuvered the old 6000LE across town. "It's not a date," he told himself in the mirror, desperately trying to manage expectations. "It's not a date, okay? It's definitely, definitely not a date."

Ten minutes later, Abby was climbing into the passenger seat of his car. "Take me somewhere good," she teased him. "Take me to the best date spot in all of Templar."

Simon immediately sat up straighter in his seat, his eyes suddenly set on high alert. "Is this a date?" he asked, and his voice squeaked as he said it.

Abby laughed, but not unkindly. "I don't know," she said. "Is it *not* a date?"

Simon's palms suddenly felt too wet to get a good grip on the wheel. "Do you want it to be a date?" he asked, trying to keep the hopeful tremor out of his voice.

"Do *you* want it to be a date?" she replied.

Simon set his lips into a hard line. He wished she would stop answering his questions with questions.

"I just—I don't—" He tried to make words come out of his mouth in some way that made sense, but it wasn't working. "You're not—we could—I thought—"

Abby laughed again, louder, but sweetly, and gently. It was the sound of glasses clinking together in a toast. "Relax, Simon. I'm just messing with you," she said, her eyes bright and warm behind her glasses.

"Oh." Simon exhaled, and then he laughed, too, a much more awkward sound by comparison. "Right."

"I already know you want it to be a date. I saw it on the big screen," she teased.

Simon stopped laughing. His face flushed dark red with embarrassment. "That wasn't—" he began.

She smiled and put her hand on his arm, just below his elbow. "Simon, I think it's sweet. I think *you're* sweet."

Simon chanced a look over at the passenger seat. "You do?" he asked.

"Yes," she smiled. "It's a date, and I hope you're taking me someplace good."

Simon smiled. "Well...I *do* know this place called Lookout Point."

CHAPTER 10

Abby looked out the window of the parked Pontiac, at the line of other cars that were also parked along the edge of the cliff that overlooked the city. "Did you just bring me to a make-out spot?"

Lookout Point was a scenic overlook high up on the side of a mountain about five miles east of Templar city limits. During the day, it was a tourist stop, a place for visitors and passers-by to pull off to the side of the road, park their cars, stretch their legs, and snap a few pictures of the sweeping vista. From the parking area, you could see almost the entirety of Templar, including both of the rivers that ran through the city, and the high green peaks of the Appalachians that curved to the south. By day, it was a state treasure…but at night, it was a hotspot for young couples to park their cars, shut off the lights, and spend a little time steaming up the windows.

Simon decided his face was just going to have to exist in a permanent state of blush now. "It's a scenic overlook," he said, answering honestly.

Abby pointed at the car next to them. "Their windows are fogged up," she said. Then she pointed at the car next to that one. "And *their* windows are fogged up. And *their* windows are fogged up. And—"

"I get it, I get it," Simon said. "It *is* a make-out spot, I guess. But that's *not* why I brought you here," he added quickly. "It's just…you're new to town, and I thought…you might like to see Templar." He gestured through the windshield at the twinkling lights of the city below. "You know. All of it."

Abby gave him a smirk. "Did Virgil give you that line?" she asked.

"No," he lied.

A tendril of Abby's purple hair had broken loose from her ponytail, and she tucked it back behind her ear. The moonlight coming in through the car window made her pale skin seem to glow. She looked otherworldly, like an angel sent to Earth to bring him both warmth and torment. He wanted to reach out, to touch her skin, to prove to himself that she was real, and that she was really there, with him, and that she was *really* Abby, and not a well-crafted string-monster facsimile of Abby knitted together by a pubescent redheaded teenager with a demon in his basement.

"What're you thinking?" Abby asked him.

Simon snapped back into the moment. "What?" he responded.

Abby laughed and shook her head, rolling her eyes playfully. "Never mind," she said. She reached down and popped open the car door. The interior of the Pontiac flooded with light, and Simon had to squint against the sudden glare in the darkness. "Well, we're here to see Templar, right? Come on, then. Show me Templar." Abby stepped out of the car and closed the door. She walked up to the front of the car and sat on the hood.

Simon joined her after fumbling with his own door handle, and he leaned against the bumper, misjudging the angle and nearly sliding right off the grill. Abby stifled a laugh.

"This is going well," Simon mumbled.

But Abby placed her hand on his shoulder and said, "It *is* going well."

Simon smiled gratefully. He looked down at her hand and noticed she wasn't wearing her gloves. "Is that…uncomfortable? For you?" He didn't completely understand the ins and outs of what it meant to be an empath, but he was pretty sure she couldn't turn it off.

"You mean touching you? Feeling your emotions?"

"Well, I mean touching *anyone*, I guess. Is it…hard? Do you *always* feel them?"

Abby withdrew her hand and placed it in her own lap. She looked down at her open palm thoughtfully, and, Simon thought, a little sadly. "Almost always, when I'm not wearing the gloves. Clothes dull it a little…skin-to-skin contact is the most intense. A lot of times, it's too much. But through clothes, it isn't bad. I actually almost can't feel anything through wool," she said, nodding at his jacket.

"Really?" Simon asked, surprised.

"Really. And I can't feel anything at all through metal. So if you ever want to hide your feelings, armor plating is your best bet."

Simon laughed. "I can't even begin to guess how you figured that out."

Abby smiled and nudged him with her shoulder. "You'd be shocked, the circles I used to run in," she teased.

They sat quietly on the hood, breathing deeply of the cool mountain air and enjoying the silence of the night. The teenagers in the cars around them were being surprisingly quiet for co-eds locked in the throes of high school passion.

"It's nice here," Abby said.

Simon smiled. "I'm glad you like it."

Abby squinted down at the city skyline. It had been foggy earlier in the evening, and some of the mist still remained. The specifics of the city were still a little obscured. She pointed at a tall building to the northwest. "Is that the Grimsley building?" she asked.

Simon nodded. "Yep. And over there is the library, the one with the white torch-shaped lights on the corners. You should go there sometime when it's open…it's a really cool building."

"I like libraries," Abby said.

Simon grinned. "Me too." He scooted a little closer, so that the outside of his right arm was just barely touching the outside of Abby's left arm. She didn't pull away. "And that bridge, way over there, with the green light on top, that's the Pullman Avenue bridge."

Abby followed his finger with her eyes and peered out toward the general direction of southwest. "So then the next bridge down from there is Llewyn's bridge?"

"Yep, that one right there," he said, moving his hand half an inch to the left.

"So where's your apartment?" Abby asked.

Simon squinted out toward his neighborhood. "It's back there," he said, pointing west of the main downtown area. "Our neighborhood is blocked by that skyscraper with the flashing light on top. Actually..." He craned his neck and looked out over the back of the car. The slope of the mountain across the road was dotted with trees, but they weren't so thick he couldn't see through them. "I bet we could see if it we went up the hill a bit..."

Abby hopped off the hood of the car and brushed off her jeans. "Well, what're we waiting for?" she grinned. "I was promised a full view of Templar, and I aim to get it." She ran across the street, and Simon followed, checking both ways for oncoming traffic.

"Cars come really fast around these curves, you shouldn't just run across," he called out, hurrying to the other side. But Abby was too far ahead of him to hear; she had scrambled up the hill and was already lost among the trees.

Simon climbed up after her, plunging in between two small fir trees. It was dark beneath the branches, and his eyes were taking a few seconds to adjust, but even though he couldn't see

Abby, he could hear her crunching over fallen branches and pine boughs. He followed the sound, his pulse racing, his heart swelling. He couldn't believe that he was here, on a date with a girl as smart, as sweet, as beautiful and magical as Abby, and that she actually seemed to *like* him. She was playful, she was powerful, and she was fearless. Simon wanted to reach out and take her hands in his hands, to pull her close, to share her warmth. He wanted her to feel his emotions through his skin, to prove that what he felt for her was real. He wanted to sink with her into a mountain clearing, smell the honey-spice smell of her skin, and kiss her in the moonlight, with the city spread out at their feet like a carpet.

He caught up to her at the edge of a clearing, but something was wrong. She wasn't moving, and she wasn't smiling anymore. She was standing as stiff as a board, her fingers stiff and curved like talons, her shoulders high and tense.

"Abby?" Simon asked, all of his elation draining from his chest in one slippery motion. It was replaced with the cold, free-fall feeling of unknown dread. "Abby, what—?" But he didn't finish the question. He didn't need to.

He saw for himself what had made her freeze.

In the center of the clearing was a circular burn mark of scorched earth. Just like the one the energy column had left behind on the football field.

"No…" Simon whispered.

Abby stepped forward. Against Simon's protestations, she held out her hand, lowering it over the burn mark in the grass. "Simon," she said, all the blood draining from her face. "It's still warm."

Simon stepped forward and placed his hand over the scorched earth, too. He could indeed feel heat radiating off of the charred grass. "This just happened," he said, puzzled.

"Probably in the last couple of hours," Abby replied.

They both stood up and jumped back from the circle, as if the energy column might return at any second.

"How is that possible? We would have seen it! Look where we are, all of Templar would have seen it!"

"Not if they're not looking," Abby replied. "We're miles away from town, and the fog was a lot thicker earlier. We missed it. Everyone missed it."

The flesh on the back of Simon's neck prickled to attention. His whole body convulsed in a shiver. "Why would she attack here? In the middle of nowhere?"

The answer came to both of them at the same time, as crystal clear as a window pane.

In perfect unison, they said, "The cars."

They turned and ran back down the hill, dodging trees and shoving aside the scratching branches. They burst out onto the road, not stopping to check for traffic this time, and barreled across the street. They ran up to one of the cars, a dark blue Camry with all of its windows covered by a thick coating of steam. "Hey!" Simon called, slapping his hand on the driver's side window. "Hey!" There was no response from inside the car. He reached down and tried the handle while Abby ran over to the next car and started beating on that car's windshield. The blue Camry was locked, and Simon moved to the next car, in the opposite direction of Abby, and they knocked on each car they came to, getting more and more desperate, trying every handle and coming up short.

Finally, Abby pulled at the passenger door of a truck parked near the end of the row, and it opened. She gave a short, sharp scream at what she saw inside.

Simon ran over and joined her next to the truck. He looked up into the cab.

There was a girl in the passenger seat. Or what *used* to be a girl. Now she looked ancient, mummified, her long hair mottled and gray and plastered to the side of her skull. Her skin was yellowy, and stretched taut over her skeletal frame. She wore a St. Gerard High School letterman jacket that had been four or five sizes too big for her before she had withered away; now it draped across her shoulders like a blanket.

In the center of her chest, framed by the burgundy curtains of the jacket, was a circular, black burn mark.

CHAPTER 11

"All twelve of them?" Virgil asked, his face a pale mask of discomfort.

Virgil, Simon, and Abby were sitting at a corner table in the Dixie Diner, a little coffee-and-pie shop a few blocks from Simon and Virgil's apartment. Simon was stabbing at a piece of pecan pie with his fork, and Abby was sipping quietly on a cup of decaf. Virgil had ordered a hot chocolate and a slice of apple pie, and even though he was uncomfortable with the story Simon and Abby had relayed to him, he still seemed to manage to stomach the late-night snack fairly well.

"All twelve of them," Simon confirmed, frowning down at the dark brown mush that his pie had become. "Six cars; two people in each car. Every single one of them shriveled up. Every single one of them with a burn mark on their chest."

Virgil sipped his hot chocolate. The Dixie Diner had the best hot chocolate in town. "So what happened?" he asked.

Simon lowered his head. He was still pretty shaken up by the evening's events.

"The police came," Abby said, taking control of the story and staring into the swirling depths of her coffee. "They forced all the doors open; that's how we saw them. They were still alive, like the ones on the football field, but…*skeletal*. Just…dried up."

"The police questioned us for a while, and we told them everything we'd seen," Simon said, putting down his fork and rubbing his hands along either side of his head. "But we hadn't seen anything, really. The mark from the energy column, and then the girl in the truck. The woman in the cloak was long gone by the time we showed up."

Virgil thought about that and tried to picture the situation in his mind. "This is why I don't go on dates," he mused.

Simon shot him a harsh look. "It's not funny, Virgil."

Virgil shrank back, his cheeks flushing red. "I know. Sorry. That was…sorry."

Abby blew across the top of her mug, absent-mindedly working to cool the coffee that had already gone cold about twenty minutes ago. "What's the connection?" she asked, staring off into space. "First the football players at practice…then you two down in the tunnel…"

"That just felt like a booby trap," Simon pointed out. "It might not have anything to do with us at all."

"Then the couples at Lookout Point," Abby finished, seemingly ignoring Simon's words. "One in the city, one *under* the city, one *outside of* the city." She frowned. "It doesn't seem geographically-based."

"I think Simon's right," Virgil said, setting down his half-empty mug of hot chocolate. "I don't know why, but it felt like that. Like the attack in the tunnel was a trap. Almost like a tripwire, some magical ambush that she had set up in order to cover her tracks. Like she was setting a mousetrap or something."

Abby sighed and set her coffee down on the Formica table. "Even if that's true, what's the connection? The football players, and the people at the lookout?"

"Maybe that they're all engaged in some sort of physical activity?" Simon suggested quietly.

Virgil exhaled loudly. "Okay," he admitted, "not untrue. But what else?"

Abby suddenly straightened up in the booth. "That girl we found. She was wearing a letterman jacket, right?"

Simon nodded. "Yeah. From St. Gerard's."

"So she was in high school," Abby continued.

Virgil tilted his head and gave her a look from across the table. "Wait…do you think *all* the people at Lookout Point were in high school?" he asked.

"I don't know," Abby replied. "I didn't see any of the other ones wearing the jackets, but that's a high school thing to do, right? Drive up to the lookout, turn off the car, lock the doors, make out for a while?"

Simon blushed. "I don't think *just* high schoolers do it…"

"No, she's right," Virgil said, snapping his fingers and leaning forward in his seat. "This might be something. The football players were all in high school…if everyone at the lookout was in high school too…"

Simon furrowed his brow. "Someone's targeting teenagers?" he asked.

"It makes sense, right?" Abby asked, leaning forward in her seat, too, and sounding suddenly excited. "If you wanted to zap a bunch of teenagers, where would you look to do it? A high school, definitely. A popular make-out spot? Obviously."

"Wait," Simon said, waving his hands through the air and trying to clear his head. "Why would someone—why would *anyone*—want to kill a bunch of teenagers?"

"But she's *not* killing them," Virgil said, his eyes growing huge. "No one's actually *died* yet. Right?"

"Right," Abby confirmed.

"But that doesn't make it any clearer," Simon pointed out. He mopped his hands down his face and tried to clear his head. "So far, she's just made them seriously messed-up. Why would you go to all that trouble, and dry-shrivel someone up, and *not* kill them? I'm not saying I'm not glad they're alive, but man, think about what their lives will be like now. Withered and wasted like that. Their organs probably charred. It's awful. It's unbelievable!

It's a fate that I think might honestly be worse than death. Who would do that to someone?"

"Who would do that to *kids?*" Abby added quietly, looking down at her hands.

Simon and Virgil exchanged a look. They knew Abby was a little bit older than they were, though they didn't know how *much* older…but they, themselves, weren't too many years removed from being teenagers.

"Four or five years ago, that could have been us," Virgil said quietly, putting shape to Simon's thoughts.

"Yeah," Simon said, setting his jaw and staring into the empty space beyond the diner booth. "I know."

They sat in silence for several long minutes. The waitress came by and refilled their drinks; they hardly even noticed her. Finally, Abby spoke. "We have to figure out why someone would want to attack them."

"And how she's doing it when she doesn't even register on Llewyn's magic globe," Virgil added.

Simon made a decision. "I'm too tired to think about this tonight. Too tired, and I still just…it was bad. Seeing all those people like that today, first this morning, then again tonight. It was bad." He swallowed hard, trying to push the memories of the withered teenagers from his mind. They didn't seem to want to leave. "Tomorrow's Sunday. We have the day off from training with Llewyn. Let's say we meet at the Dark Matter office at noon and brainstorm then. See if we can figure out why she might be doing this."

Virgil and Abby both nodded.

"Those couples at Lookout Point were attacked because we haven't been fast enough to find her. We have to stop this, and before more people get hurt."

They all agreed on that point…though none of them felt confident they would find the woman before she struck again.

CHAPTER 12

Llewyn frowned down at the dusty, yellowed pages of the book. He wasn't finding answers to any of his questions.

If anything, his research was just leading to more questions.

He slammed the book closed and stood up from the table. He rubbed his eye, trying to will away the tiredness that was seeping into his bones.

He lifted up the heavy book, groaning under the weight of it. The spine of the ancient tome was eight inches wide, and it was bound with iron. He heaved the book back up onto the shelf and sighed. Then he moved on to the next book, pulled it down from the shelf, slammed it on the table, opened it up, and began to read.

He had been at it all night. The sun would be up in less than two hours, and he wasn't any closer to understanding the new threat of the cloaked woman than he had been when he started almost twelve hours before.

He had never experienced a magical being who didn't register on his globe. That meant one of two things for the woman in the cloak; either the power she had wielded wasn't magic, or she was so extraordinarily powerful that she had the ability to hide herself from his sight. If she wasn't a magical creature, then the power she wielded was science. That scared him, because Llewyn had seen an extraordinary evolution of scientific progression in his long, long life, but he had never seen any man-made tool that could create anything close to the sustained lightning column that the woman had used to attack the football players. And if she *was* a magical being…well, that scared him, too; even with the full strength of his power, he wouldn't know where to begin combatting someone as strong as she must have been.

Neither option seemed likely, but he knew that one of them must be true.

His chest itched around the edges of the black dagger that was lodged there. He scratched the skin through his shirt, and then, just as a test, he gripped the front edge of the obsidian sliver through the cotton and tried to pull it out.

It didn't budge.

It never budged.

But it was always worth a try.

The book before him now was a text on metaphysical potions, lab-made elixirs that were imbued with quantum elements that fueled them and gave them various otherworldly attributes. Because they were powered by the quantum field, they were science-based, and not magical in nature. Theoretically, then, someone could wield the powers of these metaphysical potions without registering so much as a blip on the magical scale. Metaphysical potions were extremely difficult to manufacture, and therefore were exceedingly rare.

Rare, but not altogether impossible.

Llewyn ran his thumb absently over the lump of the black blade in his chest as he read about metaphysical positions with elemental properties. He scrutinized the formula for the Whippoor-Wind potion. It had nothing to do with energy columns or lightning branches, but it was an interesting potion, nonetheless. It consisted of two main liquid components, each one a mixture of acids and bases and oxidizers and sulfides that, when mixed to the proper proportions, caused a string of chemical reactions that fired the particles to a quantum level, opening up holes in the quantum field and harnessing the elements of two distinct planes of existence. The first liquid component tapped into the Fields of Air, a super-quantum dimension that consisted wholly of hyper-concentrated, oxygenized air. The second liquid component, if mixed properly, opened a subatomic gateway into a realm of pure pressure. If the two liquids were mixed together, the pressure from the second component would funnel through the quantum openings between the particles and force the air seeping through the particles of the first liquid component, turning the combined liquids into an elemental potion that caused extremely powerful and highly uncontrollable winds.

The Whippoor-Wind potion had to be mixed in a vacuum; otherwise, the uncontrolled and explosive winds would destroy the creator. But if they could be successfully combined, and then injected into a capsule and sealed, the potion could be used for high-intensity wind bombs.

Llewyn placed a bookmark on that page. He would come back to it when the boys were ready.

He continued to skim through the metaphysical potions; Fire-Grease, Earthen Split, Watery Grave, Mists of Sand…and there were a handful potions that channeled lightning, like Strike Gel and Electro-Water, but there was no mention of any sort of concoction that could channel the raw power that he had seen play out on the YouTube video on Virgil's phone.

He closed the book, and closed his eyes. He felt very, very tired.

His chest hadn't stopped itching. He scratched at the ever-present wound as he lifted the book with his other hand and slid it back into its place on the shelf.

It was difficult not to feel the familiar anger growing in his chest when Morilan's dark blade made itself felt this way. It didn't itch often, but when it did, he was filled with rage and regret over the Carpathian battle against the evil mage. He had been so stupid, letting his shields down, and he paid for it every day now. The blade was always a source of pain and discomfort; he'd existed with it so long that the dull, ever-present pain was a part of him now. It bothered him, but he could live with it. But on the nights when the edges of his skin began to itch from the slight tremoring of the black dagger…it was the itching that drove him mad. It was too much insult added to too much injury, and it threatened to derail his concentration now.

Llewyn pulled the next book down from the shelf. He laid it on the table. He was so very, very tired.

He opened the book. He began to read.

His study was the size of a gymnasium, lined from floor to ceiling with bookshelves that were filled with books of all shapes, sizes, weights, and topics. Most of them, he had never even touched, much less read. The books contained a seemingly infinite universe of knowledge, and searching for something as unknown and obscured as the power of the woman in the cloak was like looking for a needle in an entire field of hay stacks.

Yet there was no other option.

So Llewyn turned the pages, and he forced his eyes to read.

He was about a third of the way through the book when the blue light in his right eye began to throb.

The wizard sat up straight in his chair. It had been several months since the eye had shown him anything of great importance, and he was relieved to be on the verge of receiving something now. He placed his hands flat on the table, palms down on the warm wood, and he closed his left eye, letting the light from his right eye socket fill his vision. The world flashed blue with static and light, and then the light faded, wiping away the curtain of the future and showing Llewyn a vision of How Things May Be.

In the vision of the possible future, Llewyn saw a vast field of wild grass, devoid of trees and hills beneath a purple twilight sky. Hundreds of human silhouettes were suspended in the air above the field, held in place by lightning bolts that speared their chests and continued on to the horizon in every direction. The bodies of the injured shook and convulsed silently; their mouths were open, as if to scream, but they made no sound other than the rustle of their clothing and the rubbing of their skin as their fingers twitched against each other. Bright light shot through their eyes and their open mouths, and from their fingertips, so that the entire field was filled with spotlights that swayed against the sky and against the grass.

In the center of the field stood a broad and powerful column of energy, similar to the one Llewyn had seen on the football field in the video, but with a larger circumference, and surging with even more power. It served as the base for the scores of lightning bolts that ripped through the bodies; they extended from the column like nerve endings.

But there was one figure that stood out against the others…a figure whose feet actually touched the ground, and who was not run through by a bolt of light. The figure had her back to Llewyn, and she stood well away, on the far side of the great column, but there was no mistaking her identity.

It was the woman in the purple cloak.

She was turned toward the far horizon, with her head tilted upward. In his vision, Llewyn followed the trajectory of her gaze, and he inhaled sharply when he saw what she was looking at: a trail of light that permeated the sky above, cutting through the swirling purple clouds like an illuminated sidewalk in the sky. The lit path extended far beyond the open field, and Llewyn followed it with his eye to the slight rise of a mountain range far, far in the distance.

The trail seemed to end directly above the central mountain peak. A thin shaft of light shot down from the end of the cloud path, beaming onto the top of the mountain.

Movement caught his eye, and Llewyn brought his attention back to the field before him. The woman in the cloak had turned around. She faced Llewyn now, and her hood had pulled back slightly, so that he could see her lips beneath the purple cowl.

They curled up into a cold, cruel grin.

Llewyn pulled himself back from the vision, opening his left eye and finding himself once again in his study. It was always jarring, coming out of a potential future, and he took a few seconds to collect himself, to bring himself back fully into the present. He tried to push away the mental image of the woman's vicious smile, though it was no easy task. She had seemed almost to actually *see* Llewyn, which was impossible; she was in the future, and he was in the present. Still, the smile felt calculated and directed, and that chilled him.

But he forced himself to push the image away, and to focus on the more troubling aspects of the vision.

The first was the sheer number of people who were being fried by the energy column. It had been horrific enough to see an entire football team suspended by the lightning bolts. But in the field, the hundreds of silhouettes had filled the air so thickly, they seemed almost like one solid mass.

Whatever the woman was doing to the people of Templar, she wasn't going to stop.

She was just getting warmed up.

The second thing that troubled him about the vision was the path through the clouds that led from the energy column and terminated in a beam of light in the mountains. That energy trail told him everything he needed to know about the woman, or at least about how she was carrying out her attacks.

The only question now was how to stop her.

He looked down at the table before him. The book that he had been reading before the vision took hold had been replaced with a different volume, an especially old book of animal-skin paper with crude runes drawn on the pages in blood. The book was opened to the page that Llewyn needed. He ran his finger along the ancient paper and began to translate the symbols that were written there.

He had gotten almost through the first line of text when a sharp pain shot through his chest. He closed his eyes and grunted, clutching the space below his breastbone. The itching at the edges of his wound had become a burning sensation, and he felt heat rising up from the skin across his chest. The pain still flaring through his torso, he pulled open his shirt and looked down at Morilan's blade.

His flesh was chalky and white. The edges of his eternal wound had become pink and irritated, as if newly infected. Tiny black tendrils had sprouted beneath his skin, starting at the obsidian form of the blade, spreading across his chest and up to his neck. Morilan's curse had finally burrowed deeply enough to nick the wall of his heart.

Llewyn's blood was being poisoned by the dark wizard's magic.

He stood up from the chair, but too quickly...the chair felt over backward, and Llewyn tripped over the upended legs. He fell onto the floor, knocking the wind out of his lungs. He turned over onto his side and worked to push himself to his knees. It was a great struggle; Llewyn was suddenly weak, and washed over with the sweat of fever.

Morilan's curse was working quickly now.

Llewyn forced himself to his feet, and he stumbled forward, one hand pressed down over his chest, the other groping blindly for the doorknob. He needed to get to his potions room, and fast. He could slow the spread of the disease and buy himself some time.

His vision blurred, and the room swam. His hand closed blindly on the doorknob, and he pulled open the door. It felt as if it weighed five hundred pounds. He stumbled out into the hall, staggering against the wall as the poison in his veins spread beneath his skin. Now his entire torso was covered in the black webbing; it had spread up into his cheeks and across his broad shoulders. He rocked and swayed on his feet, falling hard to the side, slamming into the far wall. He righted himself and grunted as he made his way forward, pulling against the stones of the wall for support. The fever raged through his entire body, and he felt his heart begin to burn like it was on fire.

He was two feet from the potions room when his strength gave out, and he collapsed. The floor tilted up to meet him, and he lost consciousness as the black blood crept into the vessels of his brain.

CHAPTER 13

"Hey, how was your date last night?"

Simon looked up at Virgil and blinked. "What?"

"I said, how was the date?"

"Are you serious?"

"Yeah," Virgil said. "Why?"

"We found twelve mostly-dead teenagers who had been totally shriveled up from taking magical lightning bolts through their chests...how do you *think* it was, Virgil?"

Virgil shrugged. "I'm just trying to find the bright spot in a bad situation," he said.

Simon paused. He considered that for a second. "It was actually really great, up until the bad part," he decided.

"Nice," Virgil smiled.

They were sitting inside the new office. They had brought over a few chairs from their apartment, and Simon had set one up behind a folding table that served as a makeshift desk. Virgil was perched on the edge of a clothes dryer, sitting with his legs crossed like a man in search of enlightenment. He reached into his pocket and pulled out a small handful of Skittles. He popped them into his mouth.

"Where'd you get those?" Simon asked.

Virgil nodded toward the stockroom in the back. "Old vending machine I found in storage."

Simon blenched. "Virg, those are probably, like, ten years old."

"Yeah, but they were free," Virgil said with a shrug. He chewed on the Skittles. They were tough as leather. But he swallowed them anyway, lest he give Simon the upper hand. "Is Abby still meeting us?" he asked. The wall on the clock said it was ten past noon.

"She should be here any minute," Simon replied. "I'm sure she—" But before he could finish the sentence, his phone rang. He pulled it out of his pocket, then showed Virgil the screen. The caller ID said *Abby*.

"Speak of the devil," Virgil said with a wink.

Simon answered the phone, his cheeks already twinging pink with the idea of talking to Abby. "Hello?" He listened carefully, and his face fell. "Get outside where?" he asked. He listened to her instructions, then he got up from his chair and headed toward the front door, motioning for Virgil to follow him. They pushed their way out into the strip mall parking lot. "Okay, what're we looking for?"

Virgil tapped him on the shoulder, and when Simon looked over, he was pointing up into the sky. "I think we're looking for that," he said.

The sky was overcast, even though there had been no rain in the forecast. The clouds were tinted purple, just like the clouds that had been over the energy column at the football field, but not quite as thick and threatening. And there was a wide trail of blueish-golden light running along the length of the clouds, as if someone had unrolled a light-up LED carpet over the top of the cloud layer, and its light was shining through the dark, swirling mist.

"What is that?" Simon asked, his voice quiet with awe.

"I have no idea," Virgil replied. "It looks like—"

But Simon shushed him. "I'm asking Abby," he hissed, and then he turned back to the phone. "Uh-huh. Uh-huh. Huh."

Virgil rolled his eyes and returned his attention to the sky. The clouds were swirling, and pretty quickly, too, almost like foam that had collected on the top of a boiling pot of noodles. And the light was shifting with it. So maybe it *wasn't* like an LED carpet unrolled over the clouds, and maybe it was more like a long raft of light that was riding the current of the roiling clouds, heading east.

"Got it," Simon said, and he hung up the phone. He pulled the car keys from his pocket and headed toward the Pontiac. "Come on."

"Where are we going?" Virgil shouted, running after him to keep up. "What's with the cloud-light? Did she say?"

"Yeah. She said." Simon jumped into the car, and Virgil wasn't far behind. They pulled out of the parking lot and headed toward the eastern side of town. "There's another energy column, this one at the skating rink over on Newstead."

"The skating rink?" Virgil said, screwing up his face. "That place is still open?"

"Apparently."

"Gross."

Simon ignored the color commentary and continued on with his explanation. "She said the column is running right through the roof, and all the windows are flashing from the lightning strikes inside. It's happening again." He turned the car onto the Interstate 85 on-ramp and pressed down on the gas. "The light in the sky," he said, nodding upward and indicating the beam of blueish-gold light above the clouds, "is connected to it."

Virgil frowned. "It's *connected* to it?" he asked.

"Yes. The path of light is connected to the energy column."

"Is that…normal?" Virgil asked.

"Is *any* of it normal?" Simon shot back.

"Well, you know what I mean."

Simon sighed. "I don't know. I don't remember seeing something like it at the high school. Do you?"

"No," Virgil said, shaking his head, "and it's not in the video, either. I've watched that thing a million times." He looked out the window and up at the cloudy sky. "But the clouds were a lot darker then…a lot thicker. It's kind of hard to see the light right now as it is. If the clouds are thick enough, they probably hide the trail."

"Okay, then. Great. It may or may not be normal," Simon said. He pulled the Pontiac over into the far right lane and took the interchange, arcing the direction of the car from northeast to east. Now they were more or less following the light path away from the skating rink.

"So I hate to ask this," Virgil said glumly, "because I'm positive I'm not going to like the answer…but where are we going right now?"

Simon gritted his teeth. He peered up at the light path through the windshield. "We're following the trail," he said. "See if we can find where it leads."

Virgil nodded mournfully. "I was afraid you'd say that."

They drove on, trading the 85 for the 76, the highway that ran through the Bypass Mountains and bisected the Appalachians, connecting Templar to Harrisburg some three hours away. The foothills of the Bypass front range rose up before them, and as they snaked through the hills, the light beam overhead dodged in and out of view, hidden now and then by the trees and the sharply-angled mountains. Every time they lost sight of it, Simon worried that the light had disappeared, but it always came back when they went around a curve or came into a wide valley.

"It looks like it runs over the Stocks," Virgil observed. The Stocks were a pair of mountain peaks that stood side-by-side with their tops leveled mostly flat by time and wind. The valley between them was almost a perfect semi-circle, so that when taken as a whole from a distance, the two peaks and the valley between them looked like the bottom half of the Medieval torture device. Despite its macabre name—or maybe because of it, Templar being what it was—the Stocks was a popular camping destination for the people in the city and the surrounding suburbs. Simon and Virgil had camped there dozens of times themselves, and they knew that part of the mountain range pretty well.

"It doesn't just run over the Stocks," Simon surmised, glancing ahead, toward the horizon. "It looks like it *ends* over the Stocks. Look." He pointed toward the northern side of the valley slope. Far in the distance, far enough that they could barely distinguish it, there was a thin beam of light that came down from the cloud trail and shot toward the earth.

"The end of the rainbow," Virgil muttered, his pulse quickening. "Except in this case, the rainbow is a lightway of evil magic, and the leprechaun is a woman in a purple cloak, and the pot of gold is—I'm just guessing here—our doom?"

"You know you don't always have to say *all* the words that come into your head, right? You can just say *some* of them sometimes and let the rest just stay in your brain."

"And deprive the world of my wit? Never."

Simon exited the interstate and pulled onto the winding state road that ran alongside the northern end of the Stocks. The weather had taken a turn toward winter in the last couple of weeks, and the mountain was littered with the vehicles of Templarians who had made the drive out to see the autumn colors of the leaves one last time. But even though the light trail ran directly over their heads on this part of the Stocks, none of the sightseers seemed to notice it; their eyes were glued to the branches, and didn't seem to go any higher.

"How can everyone be so calm and cool about this?" Virgil demanded. "That light is frying the life out of a bunch of dorks at the skating rink *as we speak*, and they're just carrying on with their holly jolly weekend!"

Simon had been thinking that too. It filled him with sadness, and with a feeling of hopelessness, every time the people of Templar closed their eyes and turned their heads from the supernatural horrors that sometimes plagued the town. He wondered—not for the first time, and not even for the hundredth time—if Laura would still be alive had the people of Templar committed to opening their eyes and fighting back against the darkness. "It's too hard to accept it," he said quietly, watching a family of three laughing and pointing up at the bright orange leaves of a maple tree as the Pontiac rumbled past. "If you can ignore it, it doesn't exist."

Virgil snorted. "Tell that to the West Templar football team."

They drove on, and the higher they climbed along the mountain, the more the cars thinned out. Most of the good deciduous trees were on the lower half of the mountain; the higher they went, the more the scenery gave itself over to evergreens, so the leaf-watchers stayed toward the bottom. Soon, they were the only car on the road.

Their phones vibrated, and Virgil pulled his out of his pocket. "It's Abby," he said, reading the group text. "She's going to swing by Llewyn's to grab the manacles, then she'll meet us out here."

"Good," Simon said, pulling the car over to the shoulder and turning off the engine. "Give her our coordinates; we have to go on foot from here."

They had gotten as close as they could by car, pulled up more or less even with the vertical beam of light, which was thinner and brighter than the wide energy column they had seen at the football field. It shot down into the forest to the south of the road, about halfway down the high valley slope of the Stocks.

"Give her our coordinates?" Virgil asked, giving Simon a look. "What are we, the Green Berets? I don't know our coordinates."

"Well, turn on Find My Friends so she can find us," Simon replied, annoyed. "You know what I meant."

"I'm not turning on Find My Friends, are you crazy?"

"Just turn on Find My Friends—who cares?"

"Then the government will be able to track my GPS!" Virgil cried.

"It's not the government, it's Abby!"

"And anyone else who can hack into a phone's GPS!"

"Your phone is already using GPS, anyone can hack in and get it anyway!" Simon shouted.

But Virgil crossed his arms. He was adamant. "I'm sorry, Simon, but I value my privacy too much to share it with Abby."

Simon shook his head, incredulous. "She is a friend who is bringing us magical weapons so we can face whatever evil magic is frying the life out of kids!"

Virgil just hugged his arms to his chest even more tightly. "I value my privacy," he said again.

"Then you're living in the wrong millennium," Simon snapped. He pulled out his own phone and shared his location with Abby.

"Can I ask a totally unrelated question?" Virgil said as Simon stuffed his phone back into his pocket.

Simon sighed. "What?"

"Should we just wait here until she brings the magical weapons to us so we don't go stumbling across some super-powerful life-force killing sorceress with just our bare hands, a Skee-Ball, and a mystical key?"

Simon frowned. He was grateful for the way his curio key had helped them back at Mrs. Grunberg's house when they were fighting Neil and his demon, but he often wished he had been given something more broadly useful. "Yeah, maybe that's not such a bad idea," he mused.

But just a few seconds after he said it, the light-path in the sky turned off. It disappeared quickly, the tail end of it zooming across the sky like a film reel that had reached its end. The back edge of the light trail caught up to the vertical beam, which flickered three times, and then disappeared.

The clouds dissolved, and the sky returned to normal.

"We have go to," Simon said, changing his mind and opening the door.

"Simon!" Virgil cried, pulling off his seatbelt and joining his friend outside the car. "We don't know what's waiting for us down there!"

"No, but there's a good chance *nothing* will be waiting for us down there if we wait for Abby! The spell—or whatever it is—is done. I don't think we can really count on whoever's behind this living down in the forest full-time." He hopped over the guardrail and began easing himself down the mountain slope. His shoes slid on the loose earth, and he had to reach out and grab the tree branches to keep himself from sliding. "Come on!"

Virgil sighed and grumbled under his breath. He threw his legs over the guardrail, too, and followed Simon down the hill. "This is a bad idea," he called out, taking his time with the descent.

But Simon didn't reply. He was too deep into the hillside.

The mountain and the forest had already swallowed him whole.

CHAPTER 14

Abby hopped out of her truck and jogged across River Road. "Llewyn!" she called out, before she even reached the tent that was strung up beneath the Mallard Street Bridge.

She stepped carefully but quickly down the side of the drainage ditch and approached the wizard's tent. She frowned when she got to the entrance; half of the canvas had collapsed. The far corner of the tent flapped lazily in the early autumn breeze.

"Llewyn?" she said again, stepping forward and peering into the tent. Usually, when she came by unannounced, the front gate was up, shielding the interior of the tent from any curious passersby…but today, the gate was down. She could see clearly into Llewyn's home.

She peered inside, and when her eyes adjusted to the dimness of the space, she gasped.

"Llewyn!"

Abby ran into the tent, startled by the rubble and ruin that had once been the entryway. Every time she had seen it before, it had been a grand, arching foyer, with stone walls reaching up to rich mahogany ceiling beams. But the beams had rotted away and had half-collapsed over the entrance; the stones were crumbling and soft, and the floor of the foyer was covered with a thick blanket of pulverized stone and tiny pebbles.

Abby stepped carefully through the dark entryway, stepping over the larger stones on the floor and crossing into the sitting room beyond. That space, which had so recently been a grand reception area, now lay in ruins; the double staircase that curved up to the second story had withered and cracked, and collapsed onto the floor, leaving only the bases of the stairwells, two broken, ragged things that reached up toward the roof with jagged, severed arms of wood.

Abby stepped carefully across the ruined floor, side-stepping the unraveling couch, and entered the hallway. The walls there were askew, slanting at a twenty-degree angle like a funhouse corridor. Half of the doors had vanished, and the handful that remained were hanging off their hinges. Abby poked her head into each door, calling down the dilapidated hallways for the wizard. Her voice grew more and more frantic as she pushed her way down the hall, coming up empty.

She burst through the last remaining door, holding her breath.

There was the wizard, lying face-down on the floor, a black puddle forming around his lips.

"Llewyn!"

She sprinted down the hall, sliding on the uneven stones, and came skidding to a stop near the fallen wizard. She reached under his shoulder and, grunting with the effort, managed to roll him over onto his back.

When she saw his face, she gasped and pulled away. His skin was purple and crisscrossed with a spider web of black veins. His neck and cheeks were swollen, as if he had been choked to death. His green eye was open and staring blankly at the ceiling; the blue light in his right eye had been completely extinguished, and now it was nothing but a dark, empty socket.

Tears welled up in Abby's eyes as she whispered the sorcerer's name, gingerly touching his face through her glove, feeling for warmth, but finding nothing but ice.

Then Llewyn gasped.

It was just one burst from his lungs, one heave of his chest, and then he fell silent again…but Llewyn was alive.

"Wake up. Wake up!" Abby demanded, patting his cheeks, trying not to slap him too hard, but desperate to get a reaction. "Come on, Llewyn, come on…" She knew CPR, but she didn't want to press down on his chest, fearing she might drive the dark blade that was lodged there deeper into his sternum. She pushed open his blue coat and gasped at what she saw; his white shirt was soaked through with a thick, black wetness.

She broke open the buttons and pulled it open below his throat. The black blade seemed to have melted inside his chest; it spilled out of the infected cavity, coating his skin like oil, and it was the very poison that was pumping through his veins, turning them black.

Abby shrank back in fear. "Oh, Llewyn," she whispered, her voice breaking.

He may have been alive, but he was just barely. He wouldn't stay that way for long.

Abby swallowed hard. She pulled off her gloves and set them aside. "Please let this be a good idea," she said aloud.

She hovered her hands over the wet, black wound in his chest. She closed her eyes, and she moved her lips, silently reciting a spell from memory. As the old words filled her mind, the magic took hold. Abby lowered her hands, placing them into the oily black mess. She cried out with pain as she absorbed the last, fading thoughts and feelings of the dying mage. They coated her mind with the thick veil of death, and the flavor of his emotions spread across her tongue, spoiled and sour, like rot.

But his feelings weren't all she was absorbing; she wouldn't have needed a spell for that. The magic words that she silently mouthed gave her the power to draw out something far more potent, and far more sinister. Up into the skin of her hands, along with Llewyn's thoughts and feelings, came Morilan's dark poison itself.

The thick black goo soaked into her palms and traveled up her wrists, moving up her arms like water soaking into paper. Abby gritted her teeth and tried not to scream. The black magic seared her skin from the inside. Her body immediately rejected it and tried to fight it off, but her immune system was instantly overwhelmed and overpowered, and she suddenly had chills, nausea, and fever. It was like getting the flu from the barrel of a shotgun.

Her whole body felt like it had turned to water, and her eyes rolled back in her head. The black magic was up to her shoulders now, and it began to spread along the sides of her neck. The instant fever sent her into a delirium, and when her eyes fluttered open, she saw the slimy tentacles of a kraken slithering out of Llewyn's empty eye, and suddenly they weren't in the wizard's hallway anymore, but in the water-wracked hull of a ship at sea, rolling on the angry waves of a mighty squall. The kraken pulled itself out through Llewyn's eye as she watched in horror. It opened its jaws to swallow her whole.

Then Morilan's black magic spread to her heart, and Abby collapsed on the broken stones of Llewyn's crumbling hallway.

CHAPTER 15

Llewyn was in a cold, dark place.

He opened his eyes. The world around him was a landscape of dark grays and black, and his human eye was having a hard time adjusting.

His sorcerer eye had been extinguished completely.

He was vertical, but he wasn't exactly standing. His toes were barely dragging the stone floor; he was being dangled by his wrists, which were tied together with a thick rope suspended from the ceiling.

Llewyn cast a simple unbinding spell to free his hands, but he felt nothing in his wrists except the biting pain of the rope digging into his skin.

Wherever he was, his magic was being dampened. Or perhaps it had been drained altogether.

Llewyn cursed under his breath.

Someone in the corner of the room clicked his tongue disapprovingly. "Language," the voice in the shadows said.

Llewyn would have known that voice anywhere. It sounded like airwave static, as if it were coming through the speakers of an old, hand-dialed radio that couldn't quite home in on the radio tower. Each syllable popped and squeaked, and the air around the sounds seemed to warble in and out of reception. It was a voice that was being projected far across both space and time, from the deepest, darkest pits of the dynagogical plane.

"Morilan," Llewyn snarled.

"Hello, old friend."

The dark mage stepped out from the shadows, and the chamber seemed to lighten a bit at his movement, so that Llewyn could just barely make out the all-too-familiar form of his nemesis. Morilan was tall and lean, with scarlet-purple skin. He wore a long, black robe that was cinched around his waist with a chain of jade crystal links. His fingers were three inches too long, and he kept his nails sharp. His white beard was neatly trimmed, and shaped into a narrow W from one ear to the other, with the middle point spiking sharply at his chin. His nose was slightly caved in, and his eyes were pure, milky white; he had no pupils to speak of, and no eyelids with which to blink.

Morilan had once been a human, with proper human features. But he had made many sacrifices for his dark magic, and those sacrifices had changed him.

The scar across Llewyn's lips burned at the very sight of the evil wizard.

"Welcome back," Morilan continued, in his otherworldly radio-static voice.

Llewyn snorted. "Back to where?"

"Does it not feel familiar? We are in a cave, beneath the Carpathian Mountains. I thought it fitting that we begin your ending where your ending began." Morilan glided slowly across the floor, moving without stepping, circling his dangling prisoner. His entire body flickered and shifted from time to time, a byproduct of the fact that he was not actually in the cave with Llewyn, but was projecting himself across dimensions.

"Why don't you face me in person?" Llewyn sneered. He spat at Morilan, and the mucous landed on the robe of the semi-solid projection.

Morilan frowned down at the offending substance, and he passed for a moment into full transparency. The mucous fell to the floor, and then Morilan reappeared. He clicked his tongue again. "Manners, manners," he reminded his foe, continuing his circumnavigation. "I admit, I'm surprised you managed to stave off my dark blade all these years. You must be weary, old friend."

Morilan reached out with a solidified finger and wiped a trail of sweat from the back of Llewyn's neck. He brought the finger to his lips and tasted the wizard's exhaustion. The corners of his lips curled up into a smile. "There are few things more delectable then the debilitation of your rival, don't you think so?"

"What do you want?" Llewyn grumbled.

"What do I want?" Morilan laughed. "I want *this!* I want you, captive and drained of your powers," he said gleefully. "I *have* what I want!" He flitted around the chamber and came face-to-face with Llewyn. "I could keep you alive down here for several hundred more years, you know. The dark blade spell, now that it has broken open and seeped into your blood, will preserve your body for centuries to come. As long as your heart beats, it will beat under the protection of my whim. And while your body slowly, agonizingly rots up there," the dark mage said, pointing upward, indicating the surface world, "your spirit is *here*, in these mountains, released of its magic, for the pleasure of my torment." Morilan's purple skin rippled with excitement. "It does make me wonder: how *did* you let yourself come to this?"

"It was the fastest way I could think to get a message to you," Llewyn replied.

Morilan tilted his head in curiosity. "Is that so?" he murmured. He took a step forward. "And what message is that, old friend?"

Llewyn looked up, at last, and met his enemy's blank, white stare with his one green eye. Then he pulled his head back and snapped it forward, smashing his forehead into Morilan's nose.

The dark wizard phased out of reality, but not quite quickly enough; Llewyn's brow caught enough bone that he heard a satisfying crunch before Morilan managed to make his projection immaterial. The majority of Llewyn's force passed straight through the image of Morilan's head, but that small, painful crack was more than enough to bring a smile to Llewyn's face.

Morilan's skin burned a deeper purple with anger. "Tricks and childishness!" he snapped, his voice wavering in and out of reception. Llewyn was gratified to see that even as a projection, Morilan's nose was trickling blood from the contact. "I'll tell you why you came to this," the dark wizard sneered, wiping the blood with his sleeve. "Because you wasted your magic on a pair of simpering mortal brats who make parlor games of the endless power of the universe. Because instead of saving your strength for the dark blade in your chest, you expended it on portals and visions and forest rooms and training-wheel magic. You let your heart get the better of your brain, and so your heart has paid its price."

Llewyn didn't have a cutting response for that. It was true; he had sacrificed so much of his magic by focusing it on Simon and Virgil and their training that he hadn't left himself enough strength to keep the dark blade at bay.

"I promised to train them and protect them," he said simply and quietly, his head hanging down, his long, white hair falling in tangled trestles.

"I hope it was worth your life," Morilan said, sounding pleased beneath the radio-static crackle of his voice. "Last I saw, your young apprentices were heading directly into certain death."

Llewyn's cheeks flushed with anger. It had been centuries since he'd been without the comfort of powerful magic at his beck and call, and being unable to conjure it now, when he was filled with torment and rage, and when he needed it most, gave him the distinct feeling of having an endless pit open up in his stomach, a pit into which all hope sank, never to be seen again.

He had never felt so powerless.

"Leave them alone," he said through clenched teeth.

But Morlian laughed. "I plan to," he assured his prisoner. "I won't need to lift a finger against them. They're bungling things up plenty on their own." He approached Llewyn again, more cautiously this time. "I suspect it only serves to make matters worse, knowing that the training that has allowed you to die was carried out in vain."

Llewyn opened his mouth to respond, but just as he did, he felt an invisible thread tug at the inside of his brain. It wasn't a painful sensation, but an odd and unexpected one…and then the tugging became stronger, and more frantic, and soon it wasn't just one invisible thread, but dozens of them, *hundreds* of them, pulling at the inside of his mind. As the threads began to pull, Llewyn had the distinct impression of being peeled away from a spider web, of becoming unstuck. He looked up at Morlian, and he grinned. "Better luck next time," he said.

Morilan gave him a curious look. But before he could inquire as to his prisoner's cryptic tidings, Llewyn disappeared from the cave beneath the mountains, and the air around him rushed to fill in the space he left behind, sucking together with a soft *pop*.

The evil wizard screamed with such fury that the stones around him shuddered and began to fall. His projection blinked out of existence as the cave itself collapsed.

CHAPTER 16

"I don't like this, I don't like this, I don't like this," Virgil whispered as they plunged deeper and deeper into the forest.

"Will you stop saying that?" Simon hissed. "We're not exactly defenseless, you know." He charged up his fist to prove it. It glowed a watery orange in the sunlight.

"We're not exactly experts, either," Virgil replied, before walking straight into a thin branch that Simon had pushed through and then let go. "Ow!" He closed his eyes and rubbed the pain out of his nose. "See?"

"Virgil. It's fine. It's daylight, we can see everything. If we get there and it looks dangerous, we'll turn around."

Virgil pushed through the brush and caught back up with his friend. "First of all, I don't believe that for a second," he said. "And second of all, why do people always say things are going to be okay because it's daylight? Daylight is terrifying! Chasing down a serial killer in the daylight is even worse than stumbling around with one in the pitch black, because if it's daylight, they can see you perfectly, and they can track you perfectly, and they can *murder* you perfectly. I've never understood that about horror movies."

"You think about the dumbest things," Simon muttered.

They hustled down the hill, dodging roots and rocks where they could, and stumble-sliding down the dirt slope as quietly as they were able. They broke through a thicket of trees, and Simon threw out his arm. He caught Virgil by the shoulder and pulled him back behind one of the larger trunks. "Look," he whispered, peering around the tree.

About fifty yards in the distance, they could see the rear end of a huge, white van bouncing along over the uneven terrain. It was an oversized, fifteen-passenger vehicle, and it looked like an airport shuttle. The windows were tinted, so they couldn't see how many people were sitting inside. There was no road for the van to drive along, just a wide path of dirt and beaten-down brush. It jounced along and made a broad, sweeping curve to the right. As it did, they could see bright blue letters painted on the side of the van that read FURTIVE HILLS.

"What the…?" Virgil said, his voice trailing off with curiosity.

Simon pulled out his phone, opened the camera, and zoomed in as far as the lens would go. He snapped a few pictures of the van as it disappeared between the trees, bumping down the mountain in the general direction of the valley road.

He frowned down at the images. They were blurry, and not particularly revealing. He stuffed his phone back into his pocket and did a quick scan of the area. When he was satisfied that they were alone, he stepped out from behind the tree. "Why would you take a van off-road up here?" he murmured, more to himself than to Virgil.

"And what is 'Furtive Hills'?" Virgil added, scratching his head.

"It looked like some sort of hotel shuttle," Simon suggested.

"Furtive Hills sounds like some sort of golf course for members of the Elks Club."

"Who even thinks of the Elks Club? What are you, a hundred years old?"

"I pay attention," Virgil said smugly.

The clearing before them was roughly circular, and large enough that a few dozen people could easily fit inside the space. It had been cleared by hand; the circular shape of the area was proof enough of that, along with the sawed-off tree trunks that were just about flush with the ground. The entire space was covered with footprints pressed into the soft dirt, some that looked fresh and some that looked quite a bit older.

"I don't think we're dealing with *just* the woman in the cloak," Simon said gloomily. He peered into the clearing, looking for something, *anything* besides the footprints that could give them a clue to what had happened in the space. "Hey, do you see that?" he asked, pointing toward the center of the clearing.

"What?" Virgil asked, squinting.

"That. Look. There are holes in the ground."

There were five of them, to be exact. There was one large hole in the center, about the size of a half dollar, flanked by four evenly-spaced smaller holes, so that all together, they looked like the black marks on a five of spades playing card.

"I don't see them," Virgil muttered, straining his eyes. He raised his foot, ready to step into the clearing to get a closer look, but Simon stopped him by throwing a hand against his chest.

"Wait," Simon whispered. He scanned the area once more, his entire body on high alert. "What if there are booby traps?"

"Why would there be booby traps?"

"The tunnel had a booby trap."

"The tunnel was dark. You just said everything was safer in the daylight. Do you see any tripwires?" Virgil asked, sweeping his arm toward the ground.

"I don't know, I just have this feeling…" Simon said, trailing off.

Virgil rolled his eyes. "Simon, they weren't expecting us. This is the middle of nowhere, it's not like people come traipsing through here all the time. Trust me, there are no booby traps."

He stepped into the clearing. As soon as his foot touched the earth, the air around them crackled with the sound of shattering glass.

Virgil looked down at his foot. Then he looked back up at Simon. "Okay, just to be clear—" he started. But he didn't bother finishing the statement, because Simon wasn't listening anyway. His attention was focused on the ground in front of Virgil.

The grass before him began to mound up, pushing up from beneath. Virgil stumbled backward out of the clearing as the mound became a hill, and the grass stretched and broke, giving way to soft dirt and mud that rose from the forest floor. The mound of earth grew huge, at least a full foot taller than Virgil, and it spread out to either side, until it was twice as wide as the thickest trees around them. Then the earth began to form itself into a shape, resolving into a man—a gigantic, brawny man made of mud. He had a huge, blocky jaw and burly, muscular arms. He wore a heavy pair of overalls and thick work boots, all made of mud, too. On his head, he wore an old-fashioned miner's hard hat with a lamp affixed to the front; in his hand, he carried a massive pickaxe. It was almost the size of Virgil's entire body, from end to end, and even though it was made of earth, there was no mistaking its lethal sharpness as the miner swung it around, and it whistled through the air.

"Well, this can't be good," Virgil murmured.

The miner swung the pickaxe at Simon's head, and he ducked out of the way just in time; the pointed end caught the tree trunk next to where he was standing and struck it so hard, it ran all the way through and came out the far side, exploding through the bark. The miner yanked back on the pickaxe, ripping the tree in half. The tree tilted forward, then fell just off the clearing, crashing to the ground and sending tremors across the forest floor.

"Yeah. Definitely not good," Virgil decided.

Simon scrambled away from the miner, who glowered down at him beneath the hard hat and rumbled forward, his wide shoulders scraping through the trees. He lifted the axe above his head and brought it down hard; the sharp end struck the earth just between Simon's legs.

"Not okay!" Simon cried. He scrambled backward, then turned and pushed himself to his feet. He dodged behind a thicket as the miner lifted the axe to his shoulder, ready to strike again. Virgil's fist began to glow, and he shot out a powerful energy beam that exploded through the miner's left leg, severing it completely just above the knee. It threw the mud-man off balance, but only for a second; the earth rose up beneath him and connected to his amputated leg, forming a new, strong leg.

"Am I the *only* one who can't regrow his limbs?!" Virgil cried.

The miner growled with anger and lurched toward him. He swung the pickaxe at Virgil's torso. Virgil threw up a shield and blocked the blow, but the pointed end of the blade struck through the kinesthetic orange substance and cracked the whole thing in half.

"I have *got* to get better at making these things," Virgil grumbled.

He shook out his hand, and the shield disappeared. He danced back out of the way as the miner's axe came free, just barely missing the blunt end of the mining tool as it careened through the air. He dove behind the thicket where Simon was crouched. "We have to do something," he said.

"Oh, you think?!"

They peeked over the top of the thicket. The mud-miner stood maybe twenty feet away, his feet planted. He raised the axe above his head, then he brought it down hard onto the forest floor. The earth opened up before the blade, cracking toward them like a fissure in a cartoon earthquake. Simon and Virgil dove out of the way as the ground broke open under their feet, crumbling away into a chasm that swallowed the thicket into darkness. Virgil slipped as he jumped, and the ground gave out beneath him. His feet fell into darkness, and he screamed as he reached out and grabbed the trunk of a sapling. The small tree bent forward, bowing under Virgil's weight. Virgil clung to the trunk for dear life, dangling over the pitch-black canyon. "Simon!" he cried. "Help!"

The miner was resetting himself, hoisting the heavy axe back up to his shoulder. Simon powered up his hands and shot two big energy blasts at the mud-man. The first one went wide, but the second one caught him in the shoulder, tearing a small hole in his upper arm. The miner reeled back a couple of steps as more mud crept up from the forest floor, flowed over his body, and filled in the gap in his bicep. It was only a few seconds of distraction, but it was enough. Simon ran and leapt over the chasm, skidding to a stop on the far side. He grabbed Virgil by the arms and dragged him up, back onto solid ground.

"Thanks," Virgil breathed.

"I have an idea," Simon replied. He outlined his plan as the miner mended his arm and lumbered back toward them. "Think it'll work?" Simon asked when he was finished.

"Not really," Virgil admitted.

"Great, let's try it."

"Sure, why not."

Simon gave his friend a hard pat on the shoulder, and they nodded at each other. It was a last, unspoken goodbye, in case the plan didn't work. Then Simon ran off through the trees, circling wide around the clearing.

The mud-miner watched him go, but ultimately decided that Virgil was the easier prey. Virgil was perched near the edge of the crevice that the miner had opened in the earth, which put him in a perilous position. The miner growled, gritting his earthen teeth, and lumbered over toward Virgil, swinging the pickaxe to knock down the smaller trees in his way. The miner opened his other hand, calling up more mud and dirt from the ground below. It flowed up his body and collected in his palm, forming into a second axe. The miner gave the new tool a few practice swings, then he held both axes up and smashed them together.

Even though they were made of earth, their heavy blades rang out like metal, and Virgil suddenly felt the urge to wet himself.

"This had better work," he grumbled under his breath.

He backed away from the miner, watching from the corner of his eye as Simon edged around the trees. Once Simon was safely out of the mud-miner's vision, he cut into the clearing, sprinting to the far edge until he stood directly behind the earth-creature. He waved his hands at Virgil, and Virgil nodded.

Here goes nothing, he thought.

He still had enough safe distance between himself and the miner, and he closed his eyes and accessed his psychic vault. He spun the dial open in his mind, opened the door, and retrieved Gladys from her spot on the shelf. When he opened his eyes again, the weathered wooden ball was in his hand.

He looked up and was startled to see that the miner had closed the gap between them. The miner swung both of his pick-axes, and Virgil yelped in surprise as he tumbled backward, just out of reach of the swinging blades. They whizzed by his chest, missing him by inches. Virgil struggled up onto his elbows, and with a warrior's cry, he threw Gladys as hard as he could.

The wooden ball zipped across the forest, exploding through the miner's torso, carving a circle-shaped hole in his belly. Gladys struck with such force that the mud-miner reeled backward a few steps, and he rooted himself while the earth under his feet rippled up his legs, crawling over his waist and filling in the gap in his middle.

Meanwhile, the wooden ball careened across the clearing, heading toward Simon, flashing through the air like lightning.

Simon closed his eyes and gritted his teeth. This was the part of the plan he was least sure about. He'd never held Gladys before, much less tried to catch her at her screaming top speed. He threw up his hands and waited for the impact.

Gladys screeched to a stop just in front of his palms. She nuzzled gently into his hands, pressing against them, as timid as a kitten.

Simon opened his eyes. He was holding Gladys, and none of his bones had been broken. He exhaled with relief. "All right," he said.

Then he wound up and hurled the ball back toward Virgil.

Gladys barreled through the clearing, smashing into the small of the mud-miner's back and bursting out through the front. She careened through the trees, then slowed down and floated gently into Virgil's waiting hands. More mud crawled up from the ground, filling in the new hole, but before it could fill in all the way, Virgil fired Gladys back in Simon's direction, and she tore a new hole through the miner's chest.

Simon caught Gladys easily, then threw her back. She ripped an opening in the miner's left leg, just above his kneecap, and as soon as Virgil caught her, he fired he back again. She smashed through his ribcage, cleaving open his side before the hole in his leg could even begin to fill.

Back and forth, back and forth, Gladys zipped across the clearing, punching holes in the supernatural mud-monster. By the time he filled in one of his holes with more mud, three new holes had opened up in his body. Gladys zipped through the air with incredible speed, becoming a soft brown blur as she rocketed back and forth between the two young apprentices. Dirt and shards of earth-stone exploded from the mud-miner as the wooden ball ripped it to shreds.

Virgil snatched Gladys out of the air and held her close to his chest. The air was still and quiet as Simon and Virgil held their breath, watching the monster with trepidation.

The miner broke the stillness by bellowing in frustration as the weight of his shoulders buckled down on the holes in his body. His left leg briefly hung together by a thin sliver of mid-shin, and then it collapsed. The miner went down hard, his right leg buckling at the knee, his left arm dangling by a thin root lodged in the mud of his shoulder. His chest was more air than earth, and his right cheek had been torn away. More mud flowed up from the ground, rushing to fill in his holes, but there were too many holes to fill. The miner crumbled down into a heap of earth, perched near the edge of the crevice he'd torn open in the ground.

The dirt around the fallen miner's form continued to bubble up and ripple along the ruined form, filling in the open spaces like spackle. The miner was slowly being rebuilt from the ground up.

"Simon! Now!"

Simon had already recognized the moment and had shifted into the final step of the plan. He closed his eyes and focused his energy. He held out his hands, palms facing outward, his wrists pressed together, his fingers fanned out to either side. He grunted with effort as he pushed his energy out into his hands. The air before him sparked to life with orange light as the kinesthetic magic formed into a thick orange shield with three circles of power runes rotating oppositely around the edges. Then, with his eyes still closed and with his teeth bared, Simon tried something he had never attempted before; he curved his fingers, straining against the orange light. The edges of the kinesthetic shield gave grudgingly to Simon's force, bending slowly forward until the it was bent into a wide U-shape.

Simon opened one eye nervously, peeking down at the shield. He sighed with relief when he saw it bending.

Then he looked up, and a gleam filled his eye as he saw the mud-miner struggling to regain his footing across the clearing. With the shield held out before him, Simon broke into a full sprint. He ran directly at the miner, and somewhere along the way, he found himself opening his mouth and screaming with determination. He slammed into the mud-monster at full force, and the shield held strong. Simon pumped his legs like pistons; still screaming, he pushed with all his might. The kinesthetic shield caught the miner like a plow, its curved edges keeping him contained in the center of the shield. Simon surged forward, and the miner went skidding before him, scraping against the ground and crumbling like a pile of stones. With one last, hard push, Simon shoved the mud-miner backward, and the creature toppled backward into the open crevice. His mud clods fell in after him. The ground sensed the miner's peril; the entire earth shook, and small pieces of dirt broke free from the ground and tumbled into the crevice behind him, searching to make him whole again. So much of the shaken earth rolled into the crevice that soon it was filled to the top, and the forest floor was whole again, with the mud-miner buried deep below their feet.

Simon collapsed onto a boulder, exhausted. Virgil joined him near the edge of the trees.

"I think the clearing was booby-trapped," he panted.

Simon snorted. "No kidding," he said.

"I also think we're going to need a little help from the Scooby Gang. This whole thing might be above our pay grade."

"Yeah," Simon nodded. "Let's go see Llewyn. He'll know how to help."

CHAPTER 17

Llewyn opened his eyes. He was lying on the floor in his hallway, and the pain was excruciating.

But he couldn't dwell on the agony that was ripping apart his body.

He didn't have the time.

He groaned as he pulled himself to his feet, his legs trembling with the effort. He felt as if he'd been broadsided by a dump truck. He took in the world around him and found his infinite mansion in ruins. The walls were crumbling; the floor stones were broken. The ceiling sagged, and the doors were rotting off their hinges.

The world blurred, then split into a vision that was half-sight, half-darkness. Llewyn blinked his eye hard and brought everything back into focus.

Then he looked down at his feet, and he let out a quiet sigh of helplessness.

Abby lay in a contorted heap on the hallway floor, her arms and legs bent and frozen in mid-spasm, her skin as gray and lifeless as lead. One glance and he knew exactly what had happened: Abby had found him here, nearly dead from Morilan's dark blade, and had used her powers to draw the mystical toxin out through his pores. It was her intervention that had pulled him from the brink of death and snapped his consciousness back from the evil wizard's mortality prison beneath the Carpathian Mountains.

Abby had absorbed a lot of the black magic through her own skin...too much of it. The poison had seeped into her core, and though she was still breathing, she wouldn't last much longer against the potency of Morilan's spell.

Llewyn wheeled around and grabbed the handle of the nearest door. The door broke off its hinges, and Llewyn stumbled forward, off-balance. The door crashed to the uneven stone floor, and Llewyn tumbled through the doorway. He threw out a hand and caught himself on the jamb before he crashed to his knees. He held himself up, his arms and legs trembling, and stepped uneasily into the potions room.

The chamber was shallow but wide, almost half the length of a football field. The walls were lined with sturdy wooden shelves from floor to ceiling, and each of the shelves was filled from end to end with vials, bottles, beakers, and jars. The glass containers held liquids of all properties, colors, and viscosities. They were sorted by attribute, and Llewyn knew each of their locations by heart. But the deterioration of the mansion had caused some of the shelves to break and shift, and some of the vials had slid down and collected in jumbles at the ends of their shelves. Others had pitched off the wall altogether and smashed onto the floor. Small tendrils of steam curled up from some of the more acidic potions, while others had begun to bubble and expand. One of the potions, a teleportation serum, had ripped open a portal in the floor near the far corner, and judging by the way the bottles on that end of the wall were shaking, Llewyn guessed that the portal led to a hyper-gravity singularity on the other end. Within a month, the entire mansion would be sucked through the portal. In less than six months, it would claim all of Templar.

Given a year, the entire planet would be sucked through the spinning doorway.

Llewyn lurched into the room. He felt an unfamiliar dread knit to life in his stomach. If the potions he needed had fallen off their shelves and shattered on the floor, then all was lost. Morilan would claim his evil victory, and Llewyn would be his tortured prisoner for ages to come.

The dark magic inside of him was reassembling its strength. He could feel it pulsing in his veins, growing thicker, suffocating his blood. He inspected his chest and saw that although Abby had drawn out enough of the mystical venom to drain it away from his heart, it wouldn't stay away long. He looked down at the floor and saw what he had feared: a thin trail of oily black liquid was flowing like a rivulet into the room.

Morilan's curse was draining from Abby's pores, leaking back out through her skin like sweat, and flowing back to the object of its malevolent intent.

The inky blackness would be upon him soon, seeping back into his skin. It would join the liquid already inside of his veins, and it would return to his heart, sending him straight back to the edge of death, and to Morilan's cavern. And though a magic spell to stop it did exist, Llewyn didn't possess as much as a tenth of the strength he would have needed to cast it.

Not *nearly* as much as that.

He stepped toward the back shelf, away from the oncoming stream of poison, and his foot failed him. It fell limply onto its side as he settled his weight on his ankle, and his whole leg gave out. He fell down on his knee, hard, and bright lights of pain exploded in front of his eye. He cried out, but immediately set to work pulling himself back to his feet. Sweat poured down his face, and his vision kept swimming in and out of focus. He stumbled, pushing his wet, matted hair out of his eyes with a clammy wrist. He fell forward and reached out with one hand, steadying himself on the wall with his palm, nearly taking down a whole shelf of potions in his clumsiness.

He leaned forward and peered at the labels on the small vials. He tried blinking harder in an effort to clear his vision, but he was so taken with fever and fatigue that he couldn't make out the words. He moved his eyes closer to the lower shelf, and he tried to ignore the feeling of cold, wet ink he felt kiss the skin of his calf, just above the lip of his boot.

The stream of poison was upon him now.

He was running out of time.

He scanned the shelf for the potion marked "stasis," but it wasn't there. He shuffled along the wall, searching frantically, and when he took a step, he heard the crunch of a glass vial under his foot. His heart sank, and he looked down with despair to see the stasis potion crushed beneath his boot and sinking into the cracks in the stone floor.

Llewyn muttered a curse so vile that he had not used it in at least two hundred years.

He swiped clumsily at the next vial in the row, the one marked "cryo-stasis." It wasn't his best or favorite option, but he didn't have the luxury of time to be choosy. He gripped the small glass jar with its crystal-blue potion and held it close to his chest, and as he did, he could feel the heat of infection radiating through his skin. The cold, black poison continued to crawl up his leg, crossing the threshold of his waist. It wasn't even bothering to seep into a vein and let the blood flow carry it eventually to his heart; the curse was going straight for the heart itself.

He lurched back across the room, slamming into the wall, actually taking down two shelves with his shoulder this time. Jars and vials crashed all around him. Through his blurred eye, he saw the telltale bright red of the second potion he needed as it hit the ground and, mercifully, remained intact. It rolled away from his feet; when he reached out to grab it, he fell forward and hit the ground like a sack of flour. He reached out with a trembling hand and closed his fingers around the vial.

The poison was creeping up his stomach now, slithering higher like a snake. He was almost out of time.

He groaned as he struggled up to his feet once more. The room began to tilt, and he couldn't tell if it was his dizziness or if the mansion was actually collapsing. He reeled to his left and tumbled out the doorway, back into the hall. He looked down at Abby and blinked hard to get his vision straight. Most of the poison had left her body, though there was still enough to give her skin an ashen tone. He didn't envy her the sick and wrecked feeling she'd have upon fully waking. For at least three or four days, she would feel as if her body was suffering the worst flu of its life. But she was alive, and she was coming back to consciousness, and that was good fortune.

He felt the poison spread over his chest. It stabbed his skin like needles as it began to sink beneath the surface. He pulled the stopper out of the vial of bright red potion and poured the viscous liquid into his hand. He whispered to the potion, his voice thick and clotted with fever, and he prayed that the words were coming out clearly enough. Then he pressed his palm against the wall, smearing it in a circular smudge.

Then he pulled at the stopper of the second bottle. The cork had frozen against the glass; he had to use his teeth to break the rime and shimmy the stopper out. He spat the cork onto the floor just as the poison reached his heart. The inky blackness coated the beating muscle, then it began to sink in. The pain and the heat of it were unbearable.

Llewyn bellowed in agony. He had only precious seconds now. He raised the vial to his lips and tipped the blue cryo-stasis potion down his throat.

The effect was immediate. The potion crystallized against the soft tissue in his esophagus and spread its ice through his body at the speed of lightning. It covered his organs, froze the blood and poison in his veins, crackled over his skin, frosted his beard, turned his hair to ice, and even spread outward from his body, crystallizing into icicles in the air, like a frozen sunburst.

Llewyn stood against the wall, now nothing more than a rough-cut ice sculpture of a man, frozen completely solid from the inside out.

CHAPTER 18

"Did you know there are *mines* beneath our mountains?" Virgil asked, incredulous.

"Of course I know that. Everybody knows that."

Virgil frowned. "I didn't know that."

"I thought you 'paid attention,'" Simon scoffed.

"Not in history class," Virgil grumped.

They were back in Simon's old Pontiac, zooming toward the East River. Virgil was sitting in the passenger seat with his feet up on the dashboard, a habit that Simon hated, but it was a battle he learned long ago wasn't worth the effort of fighting. "I thought you were trying to get ahold of Abby," Simon pointed out.

"I tried. I've texted her, like, eight times. She's not responding."

"Why don't you try calling her?"

Virgil made a sour look with his face. "Who *calls* people?" he asked. "She's probably still at Llewyn's...he gets terrible service. So in the meantime, I'm Googling 'mud miner monsters Templar.'"

"The NSA is going to love that," Simon said, rolling his eyes.

Virgil ignored him. "It says here the mountains east of Templar used to be big coal mining territory. Most of the mines around the Stocks were owned by J. P. Grimsley, whoever that was—"

"Early 20th century heir of the ultra-rich family that founded Templar," Simon interrupted. "Geez, Virgil, you really *don't* pay attention to history. There are, like, twenty buildings in Templar named after the Grimsleys. Including the old opera house that is literally four blocks from our apartment."

"How would I know that?" Virgil asked indignantly. "I hate opera. Now listen. This says Grimsley had a whole series of mines down there, and in 1927, there was a huge collapse, and over *fifty* miners died in the cave-in." He looked up from his phone and stared thoughtfully at the road ahead. "Holy Hamburg. Do you think the woman in the cloak booby-trapped the woods with the *mud-ghost* of a poor, dead miner?"

"Virgil, of *course* I think the woman in the cloak booby-trapped the woods with the mud-ghost of a dead miner. There was never a single second where that was even a question. Of *course* she booby-trapped it with the mud-ghost of a miner, did you not see the giant mud-ghost of the miner that tried to take off your head with his pickaxe?!"

"Wow. Being summoned up as a mud-ghost to do the dirty work for some psychopath who attacks teenagers with lightning." Virgil gave a low whistle. "Talk about adding insult to injury."

"Did you find anything about Furtive Hills?" Simon asked.

"Oh, right." Virgil looked back down at his phone and began tapping the screen. After a minute or two, he frowned. "Nothing," he declared. "Like, *nothing* nothing." He looked up at Simon. "I guess they take the 'furtive' part of the name pretty seriously, huh?"

"Keep looking," Simon urged, navigating the highway. "They put the name on the side of a van, they're not exactly hiding it. There has to be *something*."

"I'm telling you, there's—" Virgil stopped himself mid-sentence. He slid his finger frantically over the screen, scrolling down the page in front of him. "Wait. Got something."

"What is it?"

Virgil held up the phone so Simon could see. "Reddit."

Simon rolled his eyes. "Find something else," he said.

"Hey, Reddit is great," Virgil replied, pulling back the phone and sounding offended. "Reddit knows things."

"Reddit thinks World War II was faked," Simon mumbled.

"You can't prove that it wasn't," Virgil pointed out. "Now listen. There's a thread by some guy from Templar who says he's seen the van a few times, up in the mountains. He thought it was weird that he couldn't find anything when he researched it, so he followed the van one time, down into the valley on the other side of the Bypass Mountains."

"This is riveting stuff," Simon sighed.

"Just listen! It's about to get good," Virgil promised. "He followed the van down into the valley, and it was really foggy. 'Intensely foggy,' he says. The Furtive Hills van disappeared into the fog, and the Redditor followed it in…and when he came out on the other end, going up the other side of the mountain, the Furtive Hills van had vanished."

Simon raised an eyebrow. "What do you mean, it vanished?"

"It says he was behind the van on one side of the valley, lost sight of it in the fog, then when he came out of the fog, there was no more van."

"So it turned off the road?"

"He says there *was* no turn-off. No other roads, no shoulder, no trails—nothing. The van just disappeared."

"Vans don't just disappear," Simon pointed out.

"Yeah, well, basements don't just pulse with red light, lightning bolts don't just shrivel up human beings, and Skee-Balls don't just go blasting through mud-ghosts, but here we are."

Simon sighed again. He sounded almost as weary as he felt. "So we have a disappearing van from a place that doesn't exist, teenagers who are brought to the brink of death by a series of targeted lightning storms, and a mysterious woman in a purple cloak who manages the whole thing and can summon up mud-ghosts even though she doesn't register as even a little bit magical on Llewyn's map."

Virgil looked up. He blinked. "Well, when you say it like that, it sounds like we're in over our heads."

"No kidding."

Simon pulled the car over along the East River viaduct, next to the Mallard Street Bridge, and got out. Virgil popped off his seatbelt and followed Simon over the lips of the concrete ditch. "I don't think this is going to make my Top Five weekends ever," he decided.

"I think it's about to fall even further down the list," Simon said, suddenly alarmed. "Look." He pointed toward Llewyn's tent.

The entire structure had collapsed into a lifeless heap of canvas, its fraying edges fluttering in the wind.

CHAPTER 19

"Llewyn?!"

They sprinted over to the fallen tarp, and Simon yanked up one of the corners. There was nothing underneath but a cold, oily slope of concrete. "Llewyn!"

Virgil pulled up another corner of the tarp. He crouched down and dove beneath it, searching frantically. But there was nothing under the tarp except the drainage ditch.

"What happened?" he cried, re-emerging from the far end of the canvas sheet.

"Llewyn!" Simon whipped the tarp around, and it came away freely in his hand, twirling in the breeze.

"Did he leave?" Virgil asked frantically.

"Why would he leave? Where would he go?" Simon snapped.

"I don't know!"

"And he's just going to leave the tarp here, dragging across the ground?"

"I don't know!" Virgil said again, throwing up his hands in helplessness.

"Llewyn!" Simon paced around the concrete slope, running his hands manically through his blond hair. His mind raced with possibilities, none of them good. "Maybe someone took them," he said, his voice high-pitched with fear.

"Took *them*?"

"Yes—them! Llewyn and Abby! Abby was coming here to see Llewyn...what if someone took Llewyn and Abby?"

"Who would come 'take' Llewyn? You can't just walk up and kidnap a wizard! You can't pull a gun and say, 'Get in the van or I'll shoot!' He's a *wizard*; he could turn the gun into a viper and have it bite the guy in the face!"

"Well, maybe they weren't *taken*, but something—" Simon froze mid-sentence. He reached out his hand and felt the air around him. "Virgil. Come feel this."

Virgil trotted forward, extending his hands, waving them slowly through the air. "What am I feeling for?"

"Right here." Simon snatched Virgil's hand and dragged it around in a circle. "Do you feel that?"

Virgil frowned at Simon. "It's cold," he said.

"It's *freezing*."

"But just right here," Virgil said. His face screwed up in confusion. "What *is* that?"

"I told you, something's not right," Simon said, shaking his head and resuming his frantic pacing. "They weren't taken... they're still in there."

Virgil started. "Still in *where?*"

"Still in the tent! Still in the mansion!" Simon exploded, throwing up his hands. "They're still *here*, it's just not...*here!*"

Virgil rolled his eyes. "Makes a lot of sense."

Simon huffed in frustration. He scanned the space beneath the bridge and noticed something he hadn't seen before. There was a length of rope stretched between two pieces of rebar that jutted out from the concrete of the bridge, likely the central line that suspended the tarp above the ground. Simon grabbed one edge of the tarp and threw it over the rope.

"What're you doing?" Virgil asked.

"I'm rebuilding the tent. Give me a hand."

They struggled with the thick canvas, pulling it down between the rope and the bridge and smoothing it across the top, from one piece of rebar to the other. Simon grabbed one edge and shook it out, making one side of the tent full and wide. Virgil ran over to the other side and did the same on that edge. With the tent reconstructed, they ran around and met at the front opening and stuck their heads inside.

There was nothing but darkness beneath the tarp.

"Come on!" Simon screamed. He stepped forward, planning to rip the canvas down from the inside in his anger, but as soon as he took a step, he smashed face-first into a solid black wall.

It was Llewyn's camouflage barrier.

The mansion was back.

Excitedly, Simon began to beat on the tangible void, slamming his fists against it and calling the wizard's name. Then something very unexpected happened: the wall splintered and cracked under the force of his hands, and then it broke away completely, shattering like glass.

"Is it…supposed to break like that?" Virgil asked.

Simon ducked into the tent, and Virgil followed. Simon gasped when he saw the state of the dwelling beneath the magical canvas.

Llewyn's mansion was in absolute ruin.

The heavy stones set into the floor were cracked and broken, their jagged edges jutting up into small, sharp crags. Some of the pieces had been pulverized to dust, as if they'd been crushed, or eroded by wind and weather over several millennia. The timber planks along the wall and ceiling were dry, brittle, and breaking away from their moorings. The chandelier in the sitting room had broken free of its chains and had crashed down onto the chest that served as the table between the couches. The thick candles stuck into the chandelier were cold and lifeless, and the heavy circular, wooden band that looped them together had splintered and broken against the chest.

The upholstery of the couches was torn, with stuffing poking out between the cracks in the leather. One of the legs of the couch nearest them had broken away completely, and the sofa tilted down at one corner. The hallway beyond the great room had actually started to collapse, with the wall caving in and creating a landslide of stone and wood and dust that extended back toward the far end of the hall.

The air was chilly, the floor was covered with a thin rime of frost, and every single thing was freezing cold to the touch.

"This is bad, right?" Virgil breathed, taking in the damage and running his hand against the cold timber on the wall. "This is…I mean, this is *really* bad."

Simon didn't respond. He was already sprinting toward the back hall. "Llewyn!" he shouted, leaping over the debris from the fallen chandelier, skidding dangerously on his landing, righting himself in the nick of time and continuing on across the broken stones. "Abby!"

Virgil hurried after him, skirting around the worst of the carnage and following Simon down the hallway. They had to go in at an angle, treading carefully over the loose rocks and bracing themselves with one hand on the slope of the caved-in stones and wood. They shimmied their way down the hall, trying every door they came to and finding them all locked. Virgil was about to suggest that Simon could try his curiocus key in one of the locks when they came to a door that stood wide open. Simon peered through the opening, and his eyes grew wide in horror.

"Abby!"

He leapt off the pile of rubble and sprinted through the doorway. Abby was lying on the floor halfway down the hall, in front of Llewyn's unmoving form, struggling to her knees as Simon rushed forward. He slid down to his knees and grabbed her shoulders, helping her up to a kneeling position. "Abby!" he said again, frantically searching her face for signs of life and lucidity. "Are you okay? What happened? Are you okay?!"

Abby looked up slowly and blinked at Simon as if she didn't recognize him. Then her eyes cleared, and something in her mind snapped back into place. "Simon," she whispered. She sighed with relief, collapsing a little and leaning into his chest for support.

Simon wrapped his arms around her and hugged her close. In stark contrast to everything else in the mansion, her skin burned with some unseen fire. Sweat matted her purple hair down in wet tendrils against her clammy forehead. Her skin was ashen and gray.

"Abby," Simon muttered, sweeping back her hair and holding her close, "what happened?"

"Uhh…Llewyn's a popsicle." Virgil prodded the cold, ice-covered wizard with one finger. The ice that encased him was several inches thick. Virgil looked down at Simon with wide, searching eyes. "This is really, really, *really* bad," he decided.

"You think?" Simon snapped. Something behind Llewyn's frozen form caught his eye. There was a smear of red on the wall that looked like blood at first, but after closer inspection, it was too bright. Plus, neither Abby nor Llewyn, as far as he could tell, was bleeding, and there were no other signs of blood in the hall.

Simon didn't know what the red smear was, but as he watched, it began to move.

The red glob spread out along the wall, melting from a sort-of circular blob into a long, thin, horizontal line. Then it trickled both up toward the ceiling and down toward the floor in thin, uneven streams.

"It's making letters," Simon said aloud. "Look."

The stain *was* forming itself into words. They watched, mesmerized, as the red line morphed into a message on the wall:

SUMMON MORGAINE.

"Summon Morgaine?" Virgil asked, wrinkling up his face in

confusion. "What does *that* mean?"

"I have no idea," Simon muttered. He shifted his weight and cradled Abby so that her shoulders were in his lap as she blinked up toward the ceiling. "Abby? Are you awake?"

Abby's eyes searched the ceiling frantically, darting in every direction. They finally moved up and settled on Simon's face, and the muscles in her jaw relaxed. "Simon," she whispered again. "You're here."

"I'm here, too," Virgil pointed out.

Simon brushed his fingers against Abby's cheek. "Abby, what happened?" he asked again, trying to keep his voice even and gentle despite the panic that filled his chest and made his heart slam against his breastbone like a sledgehammer.

Abby's eyes rolled to the side, and she peered at the frozen statue of Llewyn through bleary, clouded eyes. "The poison..." she whispered, each word coming out thick and slow. "His heart..."

"Morilan's poison? It got to Llewyn's heart?" Simon asked. Abby nodded slowly, and she winced from the pain. She closed her eyes, and she seemed to waver in and out of consciousness. Simon looked up at Virgil. "That must be why he's frozen. Something in the dark magic."

"I don't think so," Virgil said, shaking his head. "Look at Abby's hands."

Simon looked down and took one of Abby's hands gently in his own, turning it over to inspect the palm. Her skin was speckled with deep black spots. Simon's brow wrinkled in confusion and he looked back up at Virgil.

"I think she drew out the poison," Virgil said. "Or empathed it out, or whatever. Some of it, anyway. Enough to bring Llewyn back from the brink."

"He doesn't look like he's back from the brink," Simon replied.

"No, but he was back enough to get this out of the potion room." Virgil reached down and picked up the empty glass vial from the floor. He read the label aloud: "Cryo-stasis."

Simon tilted his head. "He put himself into a cryogenic stasis? Why would he do that?"

Virgil shrugged. "Maybe if he's frozen, the poison is frozen, too, and it can't move back into his heart." The glass was as cold as ice. He dropped the vial and shook some warmth back into his hand.

Simon looked back down at Abby, who was moving her lips and trembling fitfully as she swam in and out of consciousness. "You think she drew the poison out of Llewyn...and then the poison came *back out of her* to go *back* into Llewyn?"

"I don't know," Virgil said, shaking his head. "But we've got a frozen wizard, an unconscious empath with black-magic stains on her hands, and a mysterious message written on the wall in what I can only assume is some dead animal's blood."

"It's not blood; it's too bright," Simon pointed out. He shrugged out of his jacket and set it on the floor, then he carefully laid Abby down, out of his lap, so that her head rested on the jacket. He stood up and inspected the letters on the wall. "Summon Morgaine," he read aloud, murmuring the words. "How are we supposed to summon Morgaine when we don't know who Morgaine is?"

"Or *what* Morgaine is," Virgil added. "Could be a demon. Or some...I don't know...weapon or something."

Simon sighed. "Great." He peered up at Llewyn's eye through the thick wall of ice. "So what do we do?"

"We could plug in a hair dryer and thaw him out," Virgil suggested.

But Simon shook his head. "If he really froze himself to stop the poison, that would just restart it. It would probably kill him. But maybe there's something about a Morgaine in one of his books? We could start there."

Virgil groaned. He had seen Llewyn's library a few times. He knew how many books covered the shelves there, and how much work it would be to start going through them. "Or, I'll Google it." He pulled out his phone and tapped the screen. "Aw, come on," he whined. He held up the phone and showed it to Simon. "No service." He shook his phone angrily and said, "Work!"

"Yeah, that'll help," Simon said sarcastically.

"Well, we're supposed to be magical, aren't we?" Virgil demanded. He shook his phone harder and commanded, "Magically work!"

"I think phone companies only work in *black* magic," Simon said. "Just go check the library, okay? I'll be in to help in a second." He crouched down and began to tend to Abby.

Virgil sighed. "Yeah, okay. Fine." He turned and trudged down the hall, toward the library.

Meanwhile, Abby's eyes were fluttering open again, and Simon helped her sit up. She leaned back against the wall, her chest rising and falling with the struggle of breathing. "Simon," she whispered, her voice as dry and brittle as dead leaves.

"I'm here," he said, squeezing her hand. "Are you okay? I have to get you to a hospital."

But she shook her head. "No," she rasped, "I'll be fine. Just… sick. But I'll be fine." She glanced up at the frozen form of Llewyn and at the words scrawled on the wall behind his head. "We have to find Morgaine."

"We will. Virgil's in the library. We'll figure it out."

Abby moved her lips, but Simon couldn't make out the words she was whispering. He leaned in closer and motioned for her to say it again. "Virgil hates books," she said.

Simon couldn't stifle a laugh. "Yeah, he does," he agreed.

Just then, Virgil reemerged from the library, empty-handed. He had a strange look on his face, as if he didn't know quite how to word what he wanted to say. "Hey, Simon," he stammered, figuring out the delivery as he went along, "I have some good news, and some bad news."

Simon sighed. "The way the last couple days are going, I guess I should be grateful for some good news," he said. "Let's have that one first."

"Before he froze himself, it looks like Llewyn was doing some of his own research, and I think he figured out what's causing the lightning storms. There's a book in there with the page open to a diagram of something called the Refracticore. Most of the words are in some language that looks like squares and picnic tables, but there's a drawing that shows a beam of light going down into a big purple rock thing from the top, then shooting back out from the sides in a bunch of smaller lights. I think someone's using this Refracticore thing to attack the teenagers."

Simon realized his mouth was hanging open. He closed it again so he could speak. "Virgil! That's *amazingly* good news! That's *everything*! If Llewyn found what's causing it, we can use that information to stop it! Why aren't you sounding more excited?" The question struck him as extremely important, and his own excitement turned suddenly to dread. "Virgil…why aren't you sounding more excited?" he asked again, more cautiously.

"Well, that's the bad news," Virgil frowned, scratching the top of his head. "The book is open to that page, and it looks like there's more about the Refracticore on the next page, but I can't turn it. And I can't pick up the book. And I can't tear out the page. And I can't take any other books off the shelves."

Simon furrowed his brow. "Why not?"

"Because," Virgil sighed, "everything is frozen solid."

Simon blinked. "What?"

"Everything in the library is frozen solid. I mean, *solid*. I can't move anything, and I can hardly *touch* anything. I think I got frostbite," he added, frowning down at his fingers.

"Well, thaw it out!" Simon said.

"How?"

"I don't know, Virgil, breathe on it!" Simon snapped. "You've got a bunch of hot air, use it!"

"But the books aren't covered in ice!" Virgil protested. He pointed a finger at Llewyn. "They don't look like *him*. There's no ice, there's no frost, nothing! They're just cold, and frozen solid. There's no ice to thaw, they just won't *move!*"

Simon shook his head, frustrated. He planted one hand against the wall for support, and for the first time since they arrived, he actually registered the feeling of the wall...and the temperature of it.

The wall was as cold as ice.

So was the floor. He could feel the chill through the soles of his sneakers.

His face fell with the dawning of realization. "Everything is in cryo-stasis. Not just Llewyn...but *everything*. The whole mansion."

"The house is Llewyn," Abby said, her voice cracking. She licked her lips and cleared her throat. "Everything here subsists on Llewyn's magic. Llewyn freezes, the mansion freezes."

"Great," Simon grumbled. "So the information about the Refracticore and how to stop it is there, but we can't access it. Llewyn knows what it is, but we can't unfreeze him. Our manacles are in the chest, but we probably can't open it, because it's probably frozen shut. Meanwhile, the woman in the cloak has been striking at least a few times a day, so that means the next batch of teenagers will be attacked..." He made a show of looking at his wrist, even though he didn't wear a watch. "…any time now." He ran both of his hands through his hair and fought against the urge to pull it all out. "Someone tell me, are we *actually* this bad at being heroes?"

Virgil's expression turned serious. "Ninety percent of being a hero is showing up for the fight. So far, we've been pretty good about not backing down. I don't plan on changing that now. Do you?"

Simon gritted his teeth. "No," he said, his voice resolute. "I don't."

Virgil's lips curled up into a grin. "Good," he said. "Me either. So let's figure out how to Hulk-smash a Refracticore."

CHAPTER 20

The plan wasn't really much of a plan. It was more of a generally and unenthusiastically accepted course of action. Simon said as much.

"That's, like, the very definition of a plan," Virgil pointed out.

"Well, then, it's a bad plan," Simon replied sourly.

Since the books in Llewyn's library were pretty much useless in their frozen state, and since they didn't get cell service in the tent (or anywhere near the East River, really), Simon and Virgil had decided to leave the tent mansion and head to a place where they could do a little research on the Refracticore. Simon had suggested the new Dark Matter office, but Virgil had refused.

"Hard veto," he said. "That place is depressing."

"It's our office," Simon frowned.

"And someday maybe it'll be a good office. Right now it's a depressing office."

"But—"

"Does it even have wi-fi?" Virgil interrupted.

Simon considered that. "No," he admitted. "It doesn't get set up until Wednesday."

"Then forget the office. We're going somewhere where I can focus."

That was how they ended up at Squeezy Cheez.

Abby had elected to stay behind. She was still feeling shaky and feverish, and Simon didn't like leaving her alone in there, with no one except a frozen wizard to keep an eye on her. But she had insisted that they go, saying that she would try to get to the bottom of the Morgaine mystery while they figured out the secrets of the Refracticore.

"How are you going to do that?" Simon had asked. "Everything's frozen."

Abby had looked at him pointedly and said, "Books aren't the only things that tell secrets."

Simon hadn't understood what she meant, exactly. But in the end, he lost the argument, and they left her alone with the frozen wizard in the tent to learn what she could learn about the cryptic red message on the wall.

"I'm Skee-Balling," Virgil announced as they walked through the doors of the Squeezy Cheez.

Simon frowned. "I thought we were researching," he said.

"We *are* researching. Skee-Ball clears my head."

"You don't need a clear head, you need to Google 'Refracticore,'" Simon insisted.

"No, *you* Google 'Refracticore,' and I, with my extremely clear head, will let you know if you've done a good job." He trotted off toward the Skee-Ball machines, leaving Simon shaking his head. Virgil glanced at the Nerf gun hanging on the wall above the counter. He felt it leering down at him, taunting him. "Not much longer," he said to the Nerf gun through gritted teeth.

He plunked some tokens into his lucky Skee-Ball machine. His shoulders relaxed, and a smile crossed his face as he heard the familiar *rumble-rumble-rumble-plump!* of the machine releasing its store of wooden balls down the chute.

"There's something seriously wrong with you," Simon called out across the restaurant.

Virgil pretended not to hear.

Simon plopped down at their usual table. Squeezy Cheez was pretty empty, though that wasn't terribly surprising, since it was Sunday evening. Parents didn't usually bring their kids there after 6:00 on school nights. There was one rowdy table of teenagers in the other room, hooting and laughing and throwing French fries at the animatronic band. One of the diners, a bulky guy in a letterman jacket, hurled a small paper cup full of ketchup at Suzie Kablooie. It splattered against her guitar. The jock pumped both fists in the air and howled with glee before serving up a round of high-fives across the table.

Simon sighed. Maybe it wasn't the worst thing in the world for someone to be taking high schoolers down a peg, he thought.

He immediately blushed with guilt for having allowed himself such a cruel thought. "I'm sorry," he murmured quietly in the teenagers' direction. He wiped his hands down his face. The strain of the last couple of days had made him exhausted. He didn't need to take it out on some teenagers blowing off steam.

"Hey. Are you Simon?"

Simon looked up and blinked at the owner of the slow, bored voice. It was the long-haired, pimple-chinned assistant manager named Toby. Simon had seen him at the restaurant a lot, and Abby had told them a few stories about Toby's more unsavory habits, like how he prodded his zits until they bled, or how he picked lint from beneath his toenails with the little pocket knives you could win with 250 tickets. But Toby was usually hunkered down in the back room, avoiding responsibility and leaving his employees to handle all the customers. This was the first time he and Simon had actually spoken.

"Uh…yeah?" he said, caught off guard.

Toby held a small brown package between his hands. He leaned down and set it on the table. "This is for you," he said. He turned to go back to the storeroom.

"Wait," Simon said, and Toby stopped. Simon inspected the package. It was a box wrapped in plain brown paper, with no markings. "Who's it from?"

Toby shrugged. Simon had never seen someone look so uninterested in anything before. "Dunno. They just said it's for Simon Dark. They said you'd be in."

"But…no one *knew* I would be in," Simon frowned. Even *he* hadn't known that he would be in…not until they were already on their way.

"Dunno," Toby said again. He looked exhausted from so much social interaction. He hurried back around the counter, pushed his way into the storeroom, and closed the door behind him.

Simon turned the box over in his hands. It was about the size of a shoebox, but not quite as wide, and was wrapped like a Christmas present, with neatly tucked sides and a crisp paper edge down the length of the box. The package weighed only a couple of pounds at most. He lifted it up to his ear and listened for ticking or rattling or hissing or anything that would give him a clue as to the contents.

But the box was silent.

He shook it carefully between his hands, and something slid back and forth against the sides.

"Hey, Virgil," he called out, but Virgil was intensely focused on his throwing form.

Simon returned his attention to the box. He turned it onto its side and gingerly slid one finger under the Scotch tape that held down the flap. He popped it off and winced, bracing for some sort of impact or explosion.

"They're not going to booby-trap the paper," Simon reminded himself out loud. Whoever had sent him the package would want to make sure that he opened the box.

He opened the other end, and then he peeled back the tape from the long edge on the underside of the package. He pushed the paper back, and it fell away, revealing a purple box with a gold-colored lid.

He looked around, suddenly uncomfortable, feeling as if he were being watched. But Virgil was lost in his game of Skee-

Ball, Toby had disappeared into his hiding place, and the jocks couldn't have cared less about some twenty-something sitting alone near the Pop-A-Shot.

He frowned back down at the box. It sat there innocently, waiting to be opened.

Simon extended his palm and conjured up a small shield. It wasn't big enough that the people in the next room might see it, just big enough to provide a barrier between himself and whatever was inside the box, in case it was rigged. He ducked behind the bright orange light of the kinesthetic armor and reached out with a careful, trembling hand. He gripped the edge of the lid and slowly, carefully, pulled it off.

The box did not explode.

He lowered the shield and peered nervously into the box. Inside, nestled in a bed of brown tissue paper, was a purple plastic View-Master.

Simon lifted it out of the box and inspected it carefully. It was an old-fashioned model, like the one he'd had when he was a boy, a hand-me-down from when his father was a child—a solid red rectangular block with a black lever, two plastic view scopes protruding from the back, and a pair of tilted parallelograms for lenses to let the light in on the front. Unlike his old toy, it was purple with a gold lever.

And despite its classic design, it looked brand new.

There was an image reel already inside the view slot. Simon pulled it out, and it was just like the reels he remembered: a flimsy, cardboard circle with notches along the edges and tiny rectangular film panels set around the disc. He held the reel up to the light and tried to identify the pictures inside but couldn't make out any of the colored shapes. He brought the disc back down and was about to slip it back into the View-Master when he noticed the title of the reel.

His heart pumped so hard, he could feel the blood pulsing in his ears.

The words typed in the center of the reel read, *Dark/Matter: Trespass and Consequence*.

"Virgil," Simon said, but his voice caught in his throat, and it came out as a dry whisper. His entire body was suddenly filled with a cloud of dread. It billowed through him, spreading like smoke, making his limbs feel heavy, weighing him down. His shocked movements came automatically, without thought, and without being prompted. He pushed the reel back into the View-Master. He lifted the plastic toy to his eyes. He pushed down on the gold lever.

The first image was a title card, with off-white letters printed on a grainy black background. It was outlined with a thin, cream-colored frame, and the whole thing looked like a title card from a silent film. The text in the middle of the frame read, *Part I: Trespass*.

Simon clicked the gold lever again. The next image slid into place.

Simon's pounding heart stopped cold in his chest.

The picture was stylized like a stained glass window, with thick black lines separating each component; the background was fractured into small, geometric panes of blues and greens and browns. Vividly-colored trees stood at attention across the mid-ground of the image. In front of the trees sat a large, brown mound of dirt, and on either side of that stood two young men, their bodies tensed in fight-or-flight positions. They looked down at the dirt pile with fear in their eyes.

One of the young men had short, blond hair and was holding an orange shield; the other had scruffier brown hair, and he was holding a small wooden ball.

It was a painting of Simon and Virgil facing the rising mudghost on the Stocks.

The illustration began to shake in front of his eyes, and Simon realized his hands were trembling. He pushed down on the gold lever again, and the picture was whisked away to the left. It was replaced by a new illustration in the same style. In this picture, Simon was running through the trees as Virgil dove away from the downward swing of the fully-formed mud-miner ghost.

Simon clicked the lever again, and the third image showed Virgil lying on his back with his right arm extended toward the mud-miner. Gladys hung mid-air, on a frozen path toward Simon's waiting hands. The mud-ghost had a hole right through his middle, and his face was contorted into a sneer of anger.

The next frame showed Simon and Virgil standing over a crack in the earth, with the defeated mud-miner's hand reaching up through the crevice.

Simon was terrified and entranced. He couldn't tear his eyes away. He clicked the gold lever again, and the frame shifted to another title screen.

This one read, *Part II: Consequence*.

A chill trembled through Simon's bones. He didn't want to see what was next.

But he couldn't look away, and there were two more frames to go.

He pulled the lever.

Click.

CHAPTER 21

Virgil was on a tear. He hadn't played a game of Skee-Ball in almost a full week, and he was worried that he'd be rusty, but the workout with Gladys in the Stocks had paid off—not just because she had ensured the defeat of the mud-miner ghost, but also because now that his underhanded rolling arm was warmed up, he had thrown three nearly-perfect games in a row. The prize tickets were spewing out from the metal machine in a steady stream, pooling on the floor in a pile that almost reached his shins.

He was having difficulty remembering a time he'd felt so completely and utterly victorious.

"I can feel the molded plastic grip of that Nerf gun in my hands!" he proclaimed to the world as he rolled the last ball of his current game. It hopped up the ramp and plunked straight down into one of the 100 point holes without even touching the rim. He dropped another token in the slot, and as a fresh new set of wooden balls dropped down the chute, he said, "Simon, are you seeing this? Are you *seeing* this?!"

He turned around and beamed across the room at his friend, but his smile quickly faded into a frown. Simon was sitting at the table with a purple View-Master pressed against his eyes. His mouth was hanging open like he'd forgotten how his jaw worked, and he was clicking the gold lever with a slow, trembling pull that somehow gave Virgil a cold fluttering feeling in the pit of his stomach.

Virgil glanced uneasily around the room. The manager was nowhere in sight, and the only other customers were the teenagers he'd seen in the back room when they walked in.

"Where did Simon get a View-Master?" he wondered aloud. He scratched his head.

It was a pretty surprising turn of events.

Night had fallen outside, and Virgil glanced at the window, but all he could see was the well-lit reflection of the Squeezy Cheez room, with its whirling red arcade lights and multi-colored neon roping. He was about to pull his eyes away from the window when a car suddenly pulled into the parking lot, illuminating the space outside with its headlights. The window's mirror effect was broken, and in the new light, Virgil saw something that froze him in place and set the hairs on the back of his neck prickling up with alarm.

The woman in the purple cloak was standing at the window, peering inside from beneath her hood, her entire body tensed and focused completely on Simon.

"Simon," Virgil said, but his throat was dry from the panic that was washing over him, and it came out as a whisper. He swallowed hard, then he called out again, louder: "Simon!"

But Simon didn't look up. He was so lost in whatever he was seeing in the View-Master that he didn't even seem to hear Virgil.

Virgil looked back at the window, every alarm bell in his head clanging. He watched with dread as the woman's lips curled up into a smile, cruel and expectant, which could only mean one thing.

She knew what would happen if Simon continued to click through the View-Master. And she was relishing the moment.

"Simon!" Virgil shrieked.

But still, Simon didn't hear him. He was too focused on the frame in front of his eyes…even hypnotized, maybe. He had advanced past the *Consequence* image, and he was now staring at a painting that was so disturbing, his skin rippled up in goosebumps, and he lost the ability to breathe. In the picture, he was standing outside of what appeared to be a hospital. Virgil stood next to him, a frown on his face, and a single tear spilling down his cheek. As for Simon, he was positioned with his arms stretched out in front of him, almost like a mummy from the old horror movies, as if he were searching the air blindly with his hands. And in the image, he *was*…because there was a white bandage wrapped around his head, covering his eyes.

As he watched the image, with his heart hammering in his chest, the picture began to *change*. Two tiny pinpoints of red color appeared on the bandage, where his eyes were…then they grew, spreading and spreading, until the entire bandage became soaked through with red. Then small drops of blood began to fall from the bandage and spill down his cheeks.

In the View-Master image, Simon's eyes had been removed, leaving empty, bleeding sockets behind.

Simon couldn't swallow. He couldn't breathe. He couldn't move. Every drop of moisture evaporated from his mouth and from his throat, leaving him an empty husk of a person, a dry, numb desert of flesh and bone.

There was one more frame in the reel.

Simon didn't want to click the lever. He didn't want to see what was next. He wanted to put the View-Master down, smash it on the floor, rip the reel to shreds, set it on fire, burn it to ashes.

But he couldn't. He couldn't lower the plastic toy from his eyes, and he couldn't stop himself from looking at the next image in the reel.

From somewhere far, far away, he heard the ripples of Virgil's voice, as if his friend was calling out to him from the bottom of a pool. He wanted to respond. He wanted to let Virgil know he was okay.

Instead, he lifted his finger to the gold lever once more, and he began to pull it down.

"*Simon!*"

Virgil acted on pure instinct. He reached down and grabbed one of the wooden Skee-Ball balls. He wound up, took a step, and fired the ball across the room. Simon's finger pulled down at the gold lever, and just as it was starting to click, the ball smashed into his hand with a loud *crack*.

The View-Master went flying out of Simon's hands, and he howled in pain. "Ow!" he shrieked, shaking out his hand. He looked around, dazed, until his eyes finally fell on Virgil. A strange look of confusion crossed his face. "Virgil?" he asked.

Virgil didn't respond. He just exhaled with relief, doubling over, placing his hands on his knees and taking a few deep breaths.

"That was close," he whispered to himself.

"Why did you *do* that?" Simon demanded. He held his injured left hand in his right, inspecting the red welt that was already rising up above the bone there. "What's the matter with you?!"

Virgil looked up at Simon and blinked. "What?" he said. "I—well, the View-Master, it—you, like—you were in trouble. The woman…." He indicated toward the window, but the car outside had shut off its headlights, and they couldn't see anything anymore except the reflection of the room.

"That *hurt!*" Simon whined.

"Yeah, but the woman in the cloak…!" Virgil said, gesturing wildly toward the window. He looked back at Simon, bewildered, unsure how his friend could be anything less than grateful for what he'd done. But there was a small part of him that pointed out that he'd just injured his best friend's hand pretty severely on nothing more than a hunch. He let his eyes slide back across the room, to Simon's surprised and angry face, and then he lowered his gaze in embarrassment and uncertainty…and when he did, he saw something that made him catch his breath. "Simon," he whispered, raising a shaking hand and pointing at the ground by Simon's feet. "Look."

Simon glanced down at the ground. The purple View-Master lay on the ground, perfectly intact. But there was something different about it now...something chilling.

There were thin, metal blades extending from each of the viewfinders.

The last click of the lever had activated a spring that shot them through the eyepieces. Simon had pulled the lever enough to spring the trap, but Virgil's wooden ball had caught his hand just in time; the View-Master had gone flying just as the knives burst through the viewfinders.

Simon had been nanoseconds away from suffering the consequences of them having trespassed on the clearing. He had been a sliver of a breath away from losing both eyes and being rendered blind.

He suddenly felt dizzy. The world upended, and he slumped out of his chair, and onto the ground.

Virgil ran across the room, sliding to a stop next to his friend. He threw his arms around his shoulders and hugged him tight. "Man," he said, unsurprised to find that he had tears in his eyes and a lump in his throat. He took a deep breath and then laughed, because he didn't know what else to do. "That was... man. That was close."

Simon was too far gone into shock to share Virgil's demonstrations of emotion. He hugged his friend back, then pulled away and looked at him with wide, unbelieving eyes. "How did you know?" he asked.

"The woman," Virgil replied. "The woman in the cloak." He gestured to the window. "She was out there."

Then, as if on some slow, silent cue, they both turned their heads to look at the glass.

"She *is* out there," Virgil corrected himself.

They clamored to their feet and sprinted toward the front door. Another car passed through the parking lot, and they could see the shape of the woman in the cloak running across the parking lot, in the direction of the Juniata River.

"She's trying to get away!" Simon hollered.

"Not this time!" Virgil called back, running hard toward the door.

They had almost made it out of the building when the ceiling of the Squeezy Cheez shattered, and a thick pillar of lightning exploded down into the room.

CHAPTER 22

The entire world around them seemed to shatter and crack as the lightning column smashed into the restaurant and shot its sizzling bolts in every direction.

"Down!" Simon screamed. He gripped Virgil by the shoulder and pulled him down to the ground. A bolt of lightning exploded over their heads, blasting into the wall, missing them only by inches.

The bolt disappeared, and the lightning column recalibrated. It shot a new bolt across the room. It forked into two ends as it flashed through the air, one electric skewer for each of them. Virgil kicked the table in front of them, toppling it onto its side. The wooden top absorbed the electricity, and the bolt retreated. The lightning column hummed louder; it almost sounded annoyed.

"She's getting away!" Virgil cried out over the electrical din.

Simon looked back over his shoulder, out at the parking lot. Beneath a streetlamp across the street, he saw the cloaked figure of the mysterious woman slipping away down an alley.

"We have to stop her!" Virgil hollered.

But Simon shook his head. "We can't!" he yelled back. He nodded toward the far end of the room, and Virgil peeked over the edge of the table. The group of teenagers in the other room had been run through by the energy bolts. They were suspended above the floor, their feet dangling freely, beams of light shooting out from their eyes and their open, screaming mouths.

"We have to save them," Simon said. "We have to stop this."

Virgil looked helplessly out the glass doors, at the alleyway where the woman had disappeared. "But…" he began quietly.

"I know," Simon replied. "I know. But Virgil, we have to help them. That's what heroes do."

Virgil looked back at his friend. His face became hard and resolute. He gave one quick, curt nod. "That's what heroes do," he agreed. "But after we save them, I'm going after that woman, and I'm going after her *hard*."

Simon agreed through gritted teeth.

Virgil peered back over the table barrier. "Got any ideas?" he asked.

"One," Simon said. "Follow my lead."

Virgil opened his mouth to ask for specifics, but before he could make a sound, Simon was on his feet and leaping over the table.

Virgil shook his head. "Here we go," he sighed.

Simon had thrown up a powerful kinesthetic shield, reaching down into all of the pain he felt over the attack on Llewyn and Abby, all the anger he had toward the woman in the cloak for targeting the innocent of Templar, and all of his frustration, borne of his own helplessness, of the fact that he'd been powerless to stop any of it from happening. He forced all of those emotions into his magic, and the shield that formed in front of his hands was solid and thick and huge; it reached from the floor to at least a foot over his head; from side to side, it was about eight feet in length. It looked like a giant windshield, and when a bolt of the fiery-hot energy cracked out and slammed into the orange surface, the shield held strong, warding off the dark magic with a loud series of hissing, fizzing pops. "Let's go!" Simon shouted.

Virgil hopped over the table and ducked behind the safety of Simon's shield. Moving together, they walked quickly across the room, skirting the lightning column in a wide arc. Beads of sweat began to appear on Simon's forehead, evidence of the strength he was exerting as he tried to hold back the power of the evil magic. The bolt of energy followed them every step of the way, crackling with anger, desperate to break through the shield and run Simon through.

They made their way slowly across the room; the closer they got to the teenagers, the more acutely the dark magic seemed to be able to feel their intent. The electricity grew angrier, more frantic, moving like a snake, testing different parts of the shield for weakness. Simon's arms began to shake from the strain of holding the shield, and the sweat was tricking down his face now, soaking his shirt at the collar. His cheeks were red with exhaustion.

"Walk in front of them!" Virgil cried out over the sound of the electricity bolts. "I'll get them out!"

Simon nodded. They reached the suspended teenagers— seven of them in all—and he continued to press onward. The edge of his shield passed between the lightning column and the first victim, a girl in a gray and red St. Médard High School hoodie. The shield severed the energy bolt, and the girl fell to the ground in a heap. The light evaporated from her eyes and fingertips.

Virgil bent down to check her pulse. She was alive...and she was conscious, but just barely.

He looked up at Simon. "Good," he said encouragingly. "Keep going."

Simon was breathing heavily now. The energy bolt that had pierced the girl in the hoodie hadn't disappeared when he'd blocked it from entering her chest. It was still firing, still searching for its victim, and now his shield was holding off two angry lightning bolts instead of one. The shield was shaking in response to the doubled onslaught, but it was holding for the time being. Without breaking his focus on the energy column in the center of the Squeezy Cheez, Simon called out, "Faster!"

He took a three more quick steps, slicing his shield through the remaining six energy bolts in one smooth motion. Their connections to the pillar severed, and the other six teenagers fell to the ground, gasping for breath and scrabbling at the floor, trying desperately to orient themselves. As Virgil looked out over them from behind the protection of the orange shield, he noticed something strange about the seven of them: they all looked somehow...*older*. Wisps of gray streaked through their hair, and wrinkles pinched at the corners of their eyes. One of the boys had a small sprinkling of liver spots on the back of one of his hands; one of the girls had suffered a change to the skin on her cheeks...it had become thin, and looked like it was stretched so tightly that it might tear like paper.

What in the world...? he thought.

A low, guttural groan from Simon snapped Virgil back to the situation at hand. Simon was struggling; that much was painfully obvious. His shirt was soaked through, and he was now fending off not one, not two, but *eight* separate energy attacks from the lightning column. And the column itself seemed to realize what was happening. It was humming louder than ever now, buzzing angrily and sending even more force through the individual bolts that were still searching for their victims. Virgil noticed a hairline crack beginning to form in the surface of the shield.

Simon wouldn't be able to hold on much longer.

"Move!" he hollered at the fallen teens. He reached down and pulled them all to their feet, one by one. They looked at him with dazed, searching eyes. He gathered them around him closely, and in as clear and impactful a voice as he could muster, he said, "We have to go. You have to move. You have to *run*. We have to go. Okay?"

The members of the group nodded, their expressions clouded with confusion.

"I'll take it," Virgil muttered. He tapped Simon on the shoulder. "Ready!" he shouted.

Simon began to move back toward the front room, and toward the front door. Most of the high schoolers began to move with him, but a few lingered. If they didn't keep up, Simon's shield would go beyond the reach of the energy bolts, and the students from St. Médard would be run through once again. Virgil fell back and ushered them forward, urging them along with his arms and his voice, feeling suddenly like a cowboy trying to herd a clowder of drowsy cats. "Come on, come on, come on," he hissed, gathering them up and moving them ahead.

Despite their confusion and their weakened states, it didn't take long for the teenagers to feel the full weight of the danger they were in. They shook themselves back to attention and huddled forward, moving across the Squeezy Cheez behind Simon's slowly-deteriorating shield.

"Come on!" Simon yelled out as the multitude of energy blasts continued to crackle against the orange barrier. The hairline split became four hairline splits, and those splits widened into substantial cracks. "We're running out of time!"

"Bank right!" Virgil instructed. Simon did as he was told, and he pivoted to his right, cutting a hard corner and planting himself directly between the lightning column and the front door. "Now!" Virgil screamed at the teenagers, helping them toward the door. "Let's go, let's go, let's go!"

They didn't need much urging; they stumbled out the door and into the parking lot, where they scattered to the edges, some of them hiding behind parked cars, others diving into the protection of the alleys on either side of the building.

"Clear!" Virgil hollered over his shoulder. Simon's arms were shaking hard now, and his muscles were screaming with the strain of holding back the energy. He eased himself back toward the door, maintaining the strength of the shield. One of the bolts began to sizzle through the surface, and the back of the shield began to glow yellow with the light of the electric power that was about to protrude through the barrier. With one final, exasperated scream, Simon dove backward, evaporating the shield as he fell through the doorway, which Virgil held open. Simon hit the pavement hard, and Virgil shoved him with his shoulder, pushing him out of the way of the open door as the energy bolts flailed around, searching for the purchase of human flesh. They dove out of the way just in time; the energy bolts hit nothing but open air and then retreated into the fury of the lightning column.

Simon lay on the ground, his chest heaving, his skin clammy with cold sweat. "We did it," he exhaled, his voice exhausted but tinged with pride. "We saved them."

But something inside the restaurant had caught Virgil's attention. His jaw was tight, and Simon could hear the squeak of his teeth as he ground them together in frustration. "No," he muttered. "We didn't."

They looked back inside the restaurant and saw the jock with the letterman jacket cowering behind the table. In all the chaos, Virgil hadn't noticed that the boy had fallen behind, too scared to move. He was gaping at them from across the Squeezy Cheez with wide, pleading eyes. Even from the distance, they could tell he was shaking.

The lightning column seemed to sense the boy's presence. It began to move, shifting through the restaurant like a massive, destructive spotlight, blasting the roof to pieces as it sliced through the building, getting closer and closer to the boy.

"We have to get him!" Virgil cried.

Simon was slumped against the wall, breathing heavily. He raised his hands and tried to form a shield, but nothing came out through his palms but a few orange sparks. "I'm out," he panted helplessly.

Virgil nodded. "Stay here, I'll go." He raised his hand and formed a shield…but it was a smaller, circular thing with only very softly-glowing runes. He frowned down at it. It was strong, but he didn't know if it would be strong enough to keep the energy at bay.

He didn't give himself time to think it over. He plunged back into the restaurant and ran head-long into the fray.

The lightning column was still moving, slowly creeping closer and closer to the cowering jock. Virgil leapt over a fallen table, clearing it easily, but the column threw a bolt of energy his way, and he caught it just on the end of his shield. The impact was enough to throw him off his balance, and he crashed to the floor on his knee. He sucked in his breath through his teeth, wincing at the pain. "That smarts," he muttered.

He struggled back to his feet, still holding the shield out before him. He hobbled forward, trying to shake the pain out of his leg. The jock looked up at him from the other room with tears in his eyes. He opened his mouth to speak…but the lightning column shot out with ten separate, jagged energy bolts, plunging them into the high schooler's body, skewering him from top to bottom.

The boy's scream was deafening.

Brilliant white light flooded out from his eyes and mouth, and even filtered out through the very pores of his skin. The fingers of energy that pierced his body hoisted him up, raising him to the ceiling. Virgil screamed and ran forward, aiming to throw himself between the bolts and the boy, but the lightning column had one last trick up its sleeve. Another line of energy crackled out from the column, striking the roof above Virgil's head. The powerful lightning hit one of the support beams, severing it neatly in half. The beam fell down, and a section of the roof followed it, collapsing in front of Virgil, blocking his way into the next room.

The last thing Virgil saw before the rubble and debris choked off his view entirely was the electrified body of the boy, hanging limp and withered near the ceiling, with lightning bolts surging through his body as the frozen animatronic robots watched silently from the stage.

CHAPTER 23

They watched the flashing blue and red lights from across the street, and when the paramedics wheeled out a gurney with a white sheet draped over the boy's lifeless body, Virgil thought he might throw up.

"Don't throw up," Simon said, reading his thoughts. "That's the only way this gets any worse, if you puke in my car."

They were sitting in the Pontiac in a daze, watching the emergency responders try to sort out the Squeezy Cheez mess. "This doesn't *get* any worse," Virgil shot back. "This *is* the worst." He couldn't take his eyes away from the gurney as the paramedics lifted it up and slid it into the back of the ambulance. "This is as bad as it gets."

"I know," Simon said hollowly. "I'm sorry. I don't know why I said that. I'm sorry."

"I know," Virgil replied.

They sat quietly in the car for several long minutes, watching police officers seal off the area around the Squeezy Cheez with yellow tape.

"It's not supposed to be like this," Simon said, finally breaking the silence. "People aren't supposed to die."

"People die all the time," Virgil pointed out numbly.

"I mean *now*. I mean from *this*!" Simon grabbed the steering wheel, squeezing it so hard that the material squeaked. "The electricity doesn't kill people. It fries them, saps their hydration, shrivels them up, but it leaves them alive. Doctors can maybe fix it, or reverse it, or *something*, if they're alive, but it's not supposed to *kill* anyone!"

Virgil shook his head. "I don't think the woman in the cape knows the rules."

"Asag didn't kill anyone!" Simon continued, barely even hearing Virgil. "Neil didn't kill anyone!"

"Not that we *know* of," Virgil pointed out.

"People aren't supposed to die!"

"Did you think no one would *ever* die?" Virgil demanded. His voice sounded sharper than he'd meant it to, but he couldn't help it. He could still see the fear in the boy's eyes before the lightning pierced his body. "We're dealing with evil, supernatural forces, Simon! Forces strong enough to suck the life out of people. Strong enough to summon mud-monsters from beneath the ground! Strong enough to bring a powerful demon into the world, strong enough to force a kinesthetic mage of the Seventh Order to lock himself in an ice vault. Did you not think that eventually, someone would die?"

Simon lowered his eyes. When he spoke again, the words were soft, almost pleading. "I didn't think we'd be responsible."

Virgil turned to look at his friend. "Listen to me," he said, gripping Simon by the shoulder. "Don't you say that. We saved six people's lives tonight. I got careless, and I missed one, and if anything, his death is on *me*, but we saved six lives tonight, and don't you dare forget that."

Simon raised his eyes once more. They were coated over with a firm resolve. "I won't forget," he agreed. "I won't forget that we saved some lives, but I won't forget that we lost one, either." He turned the key in the ignition and started up the car.

"What're you doing?" Virgil asked. "Don't you think we should go over there and talk to the cops?"

"Later," Simon said, his voice firm. He clicked his seat belt, and Virgil did the same. "You know what the worst part of losing Laura was, besides actually losing Laura?"

Virgil sighed. "I was just thinking about her, too…" he said.

"The worst part besides losing her was not even knowing where to look for justice…not knowing who had killed her in the woods." He threw the Pontiac into drive and tore out of the parking lot. "I'm not going to forget that we lost someone tonight. And this time, I know how to avenge the dead."

Virgil raised an eyebrow at his friend. "What're you saying?" he asked.

Simon gripped the wheel and pushed his foot down on the gas. "I'm saying that enough is enough. This ends tonight."

CHAPTER 24

Abby felt like she'd died of flu and been cruelly dredged back to just this side of life. Her head burned with fever; she shivered with ice-cold chills, and her entire body was covered in a sheen of clammy sweat. Her muscles ached, her bones hurt, her throat felt dry and raw, as if she'd been swallowing sand.

"I'm never saving Llewyn again," she muttered.

By keeping both hands planted solidly against the wall, she found she could manage to walk a mostly-straight line. A quick peek inside the library confirmed what Virgil had said, that every single book in the room was frozen solid. And if the library was frozen, all of the other rooms would be frozen too, no doubt. She had no idea how she was going to get to the bottom of the "Summon Morgaine" mystery.

But she had a hunch that she would have a little easier time of it if she wasn't so deathly ill.

She inched her way back down the hall, passing one hand over the other and stopping every few steps to catch her breath. She passed by the frozen wizard and eased herself across the hall, falling down against the open doorway into the potions room. The space was a mess; broken bottles littered the floor, and a few dozen potions and salves of varying colors and consistencies were all frozen into hard puddles.

If she'd had the time and the mental acuity to consider it, she would have been overwhelmed by the sheer number of potions that were stored in the room. She gripped the door jamb and squinted at the labels she could read. She was nervous that, if she went any further into the room without the support of the door, she would collapse against the floor-to-ceiling shelves and make an even bigger mess than there already was.

She didn't know what she was looking for, exactly…any liquid potion was bound to be frozen inside its glass vial and ultimately useless to her. There were plenty of warming potions and melting potions and counter-curse potions within view, but they were no good to her in stasis. She was about to stumble back out of the potions room to explore the rest of the mansion when something in the near corner of the room caught her eye.

"Oh," she said, brightening a bit as she read the label. "Why, yes, I think that will do nicely."

She smiled with mischief and stumbled toward the jar.

CHAPTER 25

"The good news is, I found some information on the Refracticore," Virgil said as they sped along the highway.

Simon scoffed. "Let me guess what the bad news is. You found the information on Reddit."

Virgil looked down and cleared his throat. "Well, I wasn't going to tell you that part, but…"

They were careening toward the Bypass Mountains once again. Simon's plan was simple, if not exactly elegant: They would return to the Stocks, hide in the trees just off of the clearing, and sit and wait until the woman in the cloak returned.

"We don't even know that she *goes* there," Virgil pointed out. "We didn't see her there, and in fact, the only times we *have* seen her, she was somewhere *else* when the lightning thing was happening."

"Then we'll wait for the van from Furtive Hills," Simon replied.

"We don't know that *that's* there every time, either…"

"Well, we'll wait until *someone* shows up!" Simon snapped.

That had pretty much ended the conversation.

Now Virgil was poring over the information on his phone screen, quickly running his eyes over the lines of text. "Do you want to know what it says or not?"

"Sure," Simon grumbled. "Tell me what the nerds of Reddit think about the Refracticore."

"Hey, the fact that the nerds of Reddit are *aware* of the term 'Refracticore' and had a conversation about it that started way back in 2016 means they're *way* ahead of us on this thing. Now stop being a judge-box and let the collective wisdom of an entire subculture illuminate the darker corners of your supposedly superior mind."

Simon didn't reply, but he made an annoyed, impatient twirling motion with his hand.

Virgil cleared his throat and began sharing the bits of information he thought were most important. "It's a stone," he said, scrolling back up to the top of the screen. "Unearthed in a deep cave near the Euphrates River in the 16th Century by a cult of monks, according to one user. Dug up by witches, according to another. One guy said it was Warren Harding."

"Warren Harding?" Simon said. "*President* Warren Harding? In the 16th Century?"

Virgil shrugged. "In this scenario, I guess he had time-traveling abilities. There's a whole sub-Reddit about it. Do you want to hear the specifics of that?"

"I hate Reddit," Simon mumbled.

Virgil nodded. "Got it. We'll skip time travel for now, whatever...they all agree it was the Euphrates in the 1500s. No one seems to know its true origin, though theories range from Mesopotamian shaman to intergalactic pranksters. Should I go deeper with the origin theories, or...?"

"Virgil..." Simon said, rubbing his forehead with frustration.

"Okay, just checking. Anyway. It's a stone. A *big* stone. A big, precious stone, carved with lots of facets. This one user says the stone was actually set into the end of a long staff made of solid gold. He posted a drawing...look at this." Virgil held the screen up to Simon.

"I'm driving," he complained, but he glanced at the image anyway. As soon as he saw the image, his eyes grew wide with interest. "Whoa," he said.

"Yep," Virgil nodded. "The bottom of the staff has four prongs...that *plus* the staff itself would account for the indentations we saw in the dirt up on the Stocks."

"They're jamming the staff into the ground and setting up the stone like a scepter," Simon said, thinking out loud. "Interesting…"

"I guess Reddit knows a thing or two after all," Virgil said indignantly. He returned to the screen. "The Refracticore is used in groups, usually in conclaves. Which I just Googled, and it means 'secret meetings.' In case you were wondering."

"I know what 'conclaves' means," Simon pointed out.

"Cool, genius," Virgil said, rolling his eyes. "Anyway, it's used in groups because of its specific power."

"Which is?" Simon asked.

Virgil smiled smugly. "I thought you'd never ask. The Refracticore has the power to absorb, concentrate, and redistribute energy. With the right spell, the stone draws energy into the top of itself, which is shaped like a cone…and then it can shoot the energy back out, and I'm quoting here, 'in absorbable form' to the people standing around it. Because of its facets, the stone has 37 surfaces, not counting the cone on top or the flat bottom, so it can redistribute energy to up to 37 people at once." Virgil put down the phone. "If I'm being honest, I don't know exactly what any of this means, but it sounds pretty impressive."

"What kind of energy does it absorb and redistribute?" Simon asked.

"It says it depends on the spell that's cast," Virgil replied.

Simon bit his lip thoughtfully. "So it's not magical in itself… it needs a magic spell to work."

Virgil shrugged. "Sounds like it."

"But the woman in the purple cloak doesn't have any magic."

"According to Llewyn's weird X-Men map room, no," Virgil frowned.

"Hm," Simon said.

Virgil waited for him to say more, but he fell silent after that, lost deeply in thought. So Virgil continued. "There's some bad news," he said, looking down at the screen. "According to this, the Refracticore is indestructible. It's cursed or immortal or magically resilient or something, no one's really sure, but apparently there have been lots of attempts to smash the thing to pieces, and none of them worked."

"It doesn't mean we shouldn't try," Simon said quietly.

"I agree. We should *always* try to smash things up. Definitely. I'm just saying, we may need a back-up plan."

"Yeah. We probably do," Simon agreed.

They sat quietly for a few moments. Virgil was hoping that Simon would throw a back-up plan out there, but he didn't. Virgil's heart sank as he realized that Simon didn't actually *have* a plan beyond trying to destroy an indestructible magical stone.

"Well," he said, putting his phone back into his pocket and sighing at the road ahead. "Maybe something will come to us."

Simon didn't respond to that, either.

CHAPTER 26

"Look, you know I'm not one to complain," Virgil said.

Simon laughed out loud, a hard, barking sound. "Oh, you're not?" he said.

"Not when it counts," Virgil insisted. "*Never* when it counts!"

"Uh-huh," Simon said, rolling his eyes.

Virgil hesitated. "Having said that, I'd like to take a second to complain."

"Go on."

Virgil looked around at the trees, and at the way they blocked out the moonlight. The leaves looked silvery in the darkness, and the trunks appeared to be pure black. The Stocks were a creepy place at any time of day, but especially so at night. "It's dark, and I don't like it," Virgil finally spat out. "There, I said it."

"You're afraid of the dark now, too?" Simon asked.

"I'm not afraid of the dark," Virgil insisted. "I'm afraid of things that can *hide* in the dark. It's different."

"You told me, like, six hours ago that you were terrified of daylight! Now you're afraid of the dark?!"

Virgil considered that. "Maybe I'm just afraid of *woods*..." he mused thoughtfully.

"Well, you can shoot magic beams from your hands," Simon pointed out, "so I think you should be fine."

"Yeah, hey, speaking of that...you know how much better I'd feel if we had our manacles?"

"I know. But we've been over this. They're in Llewyn's chest, and it's frozen shut," Simon frowned. "We'll just have to...aim better."

Virgil grimaced. "Great," he muttered. "Also, while I'm complaining about things, it's cold out here."

"It's not that cold," Simon said.

"I can see my breath!" Virgil exhaled for emphasis, and a cloud of steam billowed out from between his lips. "It's cold, and it's dark, and it's the middle of the night, and I'm tired."

Simon checked his watch. "It's 9:17," he said.

Virgil started. "Seriously?" he asked. He looked around at the dark woods and frowned. "Man, it sure gets dark early in the fall."

"But you're not one to complain," Simon reminded him.

"I am not one to complain," Virgil agreed.

They stood in quiet contemplation for several long minutes, waiting for something to happen. Virgil rubbed his arms to keep himself warm, but Simon was too lost in thought to notice the chill in the air. "You said the Refracticore collects energy, then redistributes it?"

Virgil nodded. "According to Reddit."

Simon held his tongue on that one. Instead, he pressed on with his point. "When the lightning hits, it scorches the victims. What is it draining? Water? Moisture?"

Virgil shrugged. "Yeah, like hyper-evaporation."

Simon rubbed his chin, his face a mask of frustrated thought. "But if the Refracticore is being used to redistribute moisture, why get it from *people*? Why not just…you know… drain a river, or something?"

Virgil chewed on his bottom lip, considering the question. "That's a good point," he decided. "Let's ask the people driving up the path in that van."

A pair of headlights cut suddenly through the forest, bouncing wildly as the van bumped along over the unpaved path. Simon grabbed Virgil and pulled him to the ground just as the headlights swept over them. They crawled up behind one of the larger trees, ducking behind its cover as the van came to a squeaking stop on the other side of the clearing.

There was a string of lights running down each side of the van, and the dim glow illuminated the writing on the side: FUR-TIVE HILLS.

The door opened, and a man stepped out. His features were lost in the darkness and the shadows of the woods, but they saw him pull two objects from his pockets, each about the size and shape of a stone. The man clapped them together in front of him, and they cracked like eggs. But instead of yolk running out, two streams of liquid fire dripped down from the broken shells. They stopped in midair, just before hitting the ground, and the liquid pooled on top if itself until the two knobs of fire became thick and viscous, burning brightly, suspended above the ground with about three feet of space between them and illuminating everything around them like torches. In that new light, they could see the man more clearly; he wore a purple cloak, but unlike the mysterious woman's silk robe, this cloak seemed to be made of a rougher, uncomfortable material, like canvas. His eyes were hidden by his hood, which he had pulled up over his head, and all they could see of his face was a strong jaw with dark stubble and a shiny gleam of a scar running across his chin.

There was a symbol painted on the front of his robe in yellow paint that had dripped a little as it dried. It was a circle bisected across the middle with a horizontal line. Above the line, balanced on its point, was the outline of an upside-down triangle. Below the line was a right side-up reflection of that triangle, filled in with color. It looked sort of like a half-full hourglass inside of a ring.

The hooded man climbed back into the van. After a second, they heard the pressurized whine of hydraulics, and they watched as a small ramp slid out from the van and its end planted down on the forest floor. The hooded man stepped back out of the van, walking down the ramp, then turned and beckoned up into the vehicle, motioning for the people inside to follow him.

Simon and Virgil could see shadows moving behind the windows, lumbering slowly toward the door. Like slow, shuttered prisoners testing their freedom, they emerged, shuffling down the ramp, holding onto the safety railing and easing themselves down to the ground.

"They're...*old*," Virgil said.

The senior citizens walked slowly out of the van, using their walkers and canes for support. They crept forward in their creased pants and heavy sweaters, some of them with silver hair glinting in the moonlight, some of them flashing smooth, bald scalps as they passed through the torches and ambled into the clearing.

"Make a circle," the man in the canvas robe barked. The elderly men and women formed themselves into a ring, grunting and groaning with the effort of walking through the fallen leaves and branches.

Virgil heard one woman near their end of the clearing murmur sourly about a pain in her hip. The man next to her leaned over and whispered, "You'll be right as rain."

As the men and women of Furtive Hills spread into a circle, the man in the cloak strode to the back of the van. He opened the doors and retrieved a long bundle wrapped in gold silk. He carried it into the center of the clearing and carefully unwrapped the fabric. The elderly people encircling him craned their necks and jostled their canes so they could lean in and get a better look, and Simon and Virgil had to stand up and peek out from behind the tree in order to see what the man in the cloak was unwrapping.

They didn't really have to see it, though. They could have guessed.

As the silk fell away, the smooth, polished surface of the Refracticore caught the moonlight that filtered through the branches, reflected in its many facets.

The stone was big, much bigger than they expected. It was a little larger than a football, and it had a similar shape. Its color was deep purple, darker than an amethyst, and what light it caught was reflected in warm yellow-orange flashes. The Refracticore was set into the top of a golden staff, held securely by three sturdy prongs that curved out from the base and clamped down over the bottom half of the stone. The other end of the staff had two U-shaped stabilization crossbars that bent downward at the tips.

The man in the cloak rolled the staff over in his hands and held it up like a spear, turning slowly so all the members of the gathered assembly could see it clearly. There were several gasps and quiet moans of appreciation and awe as they gazed upon the beauty of the Refracticore. Then the man in the cloak jammed the staff into the earth, and it sank down deep into the ground.

"Behold, the moment of your great gift," the man said. It sounded to Simon as if he were repeating a memorized line; there wasn't a whole lot of passion behind the words. "You have been chosen. Let us honor the source of your deliverance and salvation." He reached out in front of himself, touching his thumbs together and tenting his fingers over them, forming a triangle with his hands just below his chest, lining it up closely to the bottom triangle in the insignia on his cloak.

He looked around at the men and women gathered there. Most of them were squinting and leaning forward, trying to make sense of his movements in the darkness. The man in the cloak cleared his throat. He jiggled his hands meaningfully, keeping the triangle intact. A few of the people around him picked up on the cue, and they formed their hands into triangles in front of their chests, too. A quiet murmur spread through the crowd as some members of the assembly nudged their neighbors and instructed them to form the triangle. One of the men on the far side of the clearing hollered, "What?" A bunch of the others shushed him.

It took a few minutes, but finally, everyone in the circle was making triangles with their hands.

"What…are they doing?" Virgil whispered. "Is this what a cult looks like?"

Simon held his finger to his lips, motioning for Virgil to be quiet. They were too close to the clearing to risk being overheard. But the look on his face made it clear that he, too, was both confused and troubled.

"Grant us your gift, lord of shades and shadow," the cloaked man continued in the same rehearsed, almost bored-sounding voice. "Power the Refracticore, and make these humble servants whole."

Nobody moved. Some of the group members shifted uncomfortably. The stillness and silence hung heavily in the air.

But then a subtle movement caught the corner of Simon's eye. He glanced over to his right, deeper into the woods, outside of the open clearing. He gasped, then clapped a hand over his mouth. Virgil shot him a look…but Simon nodded into the woods, and when Virgil looked and saw what Simon was seeing, he had to put his hand over his mouth, too, to stop from crying out.

The shadows of the trees were gathering into a puddle of darkness.

It was such a small and subtle movement that they couldn't be sure at first that it was actually what they were seeing. The moonlight was dim, so the shadows of the trees were insubstantial and hard to see against the forest floor. But they wavered, as if becoming liquid shadow-streams, and then they began to run together, slowly, connecting to each other like drops of mercury in the night.

More and more shadows came together, forming a bigger and bigger pool, and then the entire mass began to creep forward, passing over the leaves and pine needles and acorns and twigs like a dark, transparent sheet being drawn across the forest floor. The pool moved toward the clearing, pulling away completely from the trees that had cast the shadows to begin with.

Virgil looked at Simon, incredulous. Simon didn't return the look, but shook his head slowly in response, his eyes still glued to the moving shadow.

"Are you thinking what I'm thinking?" Virgil mouthed.

"The shadow-man at Mrs. Grunberg's house?" Simon breathed.

"Yeah," Virgil nodded. He stared at the flowing darkness and whispered, "Moving shadow creatures."

As the puddle approached the clearing, it split into three rivulets, like a stream, and spilled around two of the elderly women standing at the far edge; the shadow streams passed between their feet, then came back together on the inside of the clearing, reforming into a solid pool of darkness. The shadow moved toward the Refracticore, and as it did, its shape began to change. The front edge pinched in, forming four distinct fingers and a thumb, and the body of the shadow spread out behind it like an arm. The shadow hand twirled up the staff, winding its way higher until it reached the top. Then the hand expanded, quadrupling in size, and the palm closed over the stone, so Simon and Virgil could only see the dull, darkened glow of it, as if the Refracticore was shrouded in heavy smoke. The air in the clearing began to thrum with energy, and a purple light glowed to life deep within the stone's core. It grew brighter and brighter until it melted the shadow-hand away; the darkness gathered back into the arm and slid down the staff, back to the ground.

The Refracticore shone so brightly, the assembled group members had to shield their eyes. One of the men reached into his shirt pocket and pulled out a pair of oversized sunglasses that he slipped on over his eyeglasses.

The light shone from every fact of the stone, beaming through the trees and creating dazzling patterns in the leaves.

Suddenly, a piece of the greater puzzle had fallen into place for Simon. The woman in the cloak hadn't registered as magical because she *wasn't* magical. She wasn't controlling the Refracticore.

The shadow-monster was the one with all the power.

The living darkness gathered into a formless pool once again and moved across the ground like silk. It slipped out of the clearing on the far side and crept up the trunk of a wide tree, close to the man in the purple canvas cloak. As the shadow climbed the tree, it began to take on a new shape. This time, it formed into the tall, slender shadow of a man.

The man in the purple cloak held out his triangle hands toward the shadow and said, "Thank you, lord of shadows and shade."

Most of the senior citizens around the ring mimicked him, holding out their arms and mumbling their thanks to the shadow-creature.

Then, suddenly, there was a great thunderclap that shook the woods, and a brilliant beam of white light exploded out of the top of the Refracticore. It shot up into the sky, and purple-gold clouds began to roil in the stratosphere, clouding the column of energy. Virgil craned his neck and watched as a trail of light spread sideways across the sky, starting from the energy column and streaking toward the heart of Templar.

Satisfied, the shadow man returned to the forest floor. He spread himself across the leaves, back toward the trees from where he had come. The shapeless puddle gathered once more at the base of those trees, and then it separated into their shadows, solidifying until the essence of whatever spirit had possessed them had slipped away, and they were nothing but the simple shadows of trees once more.

"Turn toward the Refracticore," the man in the cloak said loudly. "The ritual begins."

CHAPTER 27

"What *is* this?" Virgil hissed.

The electric hum of the energy column was loud enough to drown out their whispers now, though the assembly in the clearing was too fixated on the purple stone to notice them anyway.

"Old people are attacking young people," Simon whispered back simply. His brain felt soft and numb around the edges. He didn't know what he had expected, but it wasn't this. It didn't make any sense. "Why are old people attacking young people?"

"Revenge," Virgil suggested. "For still being able to jump and stuff."

Simon opened his mouth to respond, but just then, a surge of power flooded back down the energy column. Simon was reminded of the time they'd watched a snake eat a mouse in biology class, and they could see the shape of the mouse as it traveled down the length of the snake's body, into its stomach. This was sort of like that, but bigger, and much, much faster.

The lump of energy shot down the length of the column, and it slammed into the Refracticore. The purple stone vibrated with the force and power of the gathered energy, and the facets of the gemstone exploded with light and power. Small, golden bolts of electricity shot out of each angled surface, firing out in all directions, finding purchase in the chests of the old people gathered around the circle.

But they didn't lift off the ground, and they didn't open their mouths to scream. Instead, they actually seemed to be *smiling*.

"What is happening?" Virgil whispered.

Simon looked on with his mouth hanging open in shock. He raised a trembling finger at one of the old men facing their direction. "Look."

The man in question was short, and stooped, hunched low over a walker, his bald head shining in the wash of golden light. The thin bolt of energy surged into his chest; as they watched, he began to straighten up, his spine stiffening, his shoulders drawing back behind his ears. He let go of the walker and stood up straight. Then hairs began to sprout on his bald head…first there were just a few scattered, growing patches, and then all at once, his entire head was growing wavy gray hair that seemed to turn darker as they watched.

Suddenly, Simon understood everything. "They're not *frying* people; they're *draining* them! They're draining the teenagers of their youth, and they're absorbing it into themselves!"

Virgil's eyes widened with the horror of realization. "They're becoming young again," he breathed.

It was more grotesque than Simon could stomach. He had to stop it.

He moved on instinct. He leapt out from behind the tree, pushed all the energy he could muster into his hand, and shot the power beam at the Refracticore. His magic missile streaked through the air and exploded against the surface of the stone, but the Refracticore didn't shatter, didn't crack, didn't so much as *vibrate*. It continued to absorb and reflect the energy of Templar's youth.

A few heads turned their way, but none of the old people moved. They could feel the life and vitality surging through their bones, and it would take more than a mere distraction to pull them away from the stream of youth that was reversing their aging.

Besides, they had the man in the cloak for protection.

He sprang into action on the far side of the clearing. He pulled another small rock from his pocket and hurled it toward Simon. Simon threw up a shield just in time, and the rock exploded against it, spilling its liquid fire across the orange surface. For a few moments, Simon held a flaming shield, until it grew too hot for his hands, and he shook the magic out of existence. When the shield disappeared, the fire did too.

"Watch out!" Virgil cried.

Simon hadn't seen the second fire-bomb coming his way. He ducked, and it narrowly missed his head. It broke open on a tree right behind him, and the flames singed his hair and turned the skin of his left ear pink. He stumbled out of the reach of the fire as Virgil grabbed Gladys from his psychic vault and hurled her across the clearing.

But preparations had been made since they had destroyed the mud-miner at the same clearing. A small but strong spell had been placed around the open ring, and when Gladys struck the space beyond the trees, she bounced off an invisible force field and rocketed back into Virgil's hand.

"Aw, come on!" Virgil cried. Meanwhile, the man in the cloak had thrown another rock bomb, and Virgil caught it with a shield of his own. "How come *he* gets to throw things across the clearing and I don't?" he demanded. He shook the shield away, then he held Gladys up in front of his face and gave her a quick pep talk. "You know what to do," he said. Then he launched the wooden ball out into the forest, away from the clearing.

Gladys zoomed through the night, dodging trees as she picked up speed. Once she'd gone far enough away from the open ground, she curved back, making a wide arc around the clearing. She came back around on the far side, coming in fast and hard, and she smashed into the cloaked man's head, knocking him unconscious. He fell to the ground, hard.

Gladys zoomed back around the clearing and settled into Virgil's open hand. "You are so much cooler than Simon's key," he decided.

"Virgil! Come on!" Simon hollered. He was running toward the clearing, where the Refracticore continued its awful magic ritual. The men and women being shot through with the energy all looked different now—younger, and healthier, their bodies aging backward through middle age. They were still too enraptured in the magic and hypnotized by the sensation of strength to pay Simon and Virgil any serious mind, and Simon slipped between two bodies easily. With a heavy shield raised, he ran into the clearing, ducking beneath energy bolts and warding off attacks of quick, popping lightning from the Refracticore as he closed in. The stone shot three streams of electricity his way, electricity that was purple and hot, not like the shimmering golden bolts that pierced the older people around him. Simon made a quick mental note: *Gold bolts are youth; purple bolts are death*. But his shield caught the attack easily and held off the deathly purple magic. He dove in, and with his free hand he grabbed the golden staff. The Refracticore sent a powerful shockwave down through the metal, and it hit Simon's hand with the force of a Mack truck. The energy slammed through his body, and Simon was lifted off of his feet and thrown backward, out of the clearing. He spun through the air as he flew, only semi-conscious, and didn't stop until he slammed into a tree at full speed. His shield took the brunt of the impact, but it shattered as soon as it struck, and the force of the collision knocked the wind from his lungs. He fell down onto the ground in a dazed and trembling heap.

"Simon!" Virgil screamed, watching his friend streak through the air and smash into the tree. He turned back to the Refracticore with fire in his eyes. He shot two quick energy bursts at the stone, but they too glanced off the surface of the Refracticore without causing damage. The stone fired back at Virgil with a bolt of purple energy. Virgil blocked it with a shield and ducked behind a tree. "Come on, come on, come on," he said to himself, his heart beating frantically in his chest. He looked up at the energy column and envisioned the matching column that was currently planted somewhere in Templar, impaling teenagers with its life-draining rays and shriveling them like centuries-old mummies from the inside out. "*Think!*"

And then three distinct and important things happened in very quick succession.

First, Virgil was struck with the realization that as soon as the ritual was finished, he and Simon would be confronted with a small army of young, strong men and women who had no problem draining the literal life out of minors and who were almost certain to serve at the murderous pleasure of the shadow-creature that restored their youth. So whatever he did to end this madness, he had to do it fast. The last thing he wanted to do was use his powers to fight for his life against a few dozen strong, healthy twenty-somethings.

The second thing that happened: while he was considering that, a tree on the other side of the clearing actually *opened*, its trunk swinging outward on a pair of hidden hinges, and the woman in the silk cloak emerged from one of her secret passageways. She stepped out into the forest, closed the door behind her, and took quick stock of the setting. She saw the man in the canvas robe lying unconscious on the ground, and her lips curled down into a hard scowl.

"Leonard," she spat, sounding annoyed. "Useless."

And the third thing that happened: she looked across the clearing, through the web-work of golden energy bolts, and saw Virgil standing there.

Virgil gulped so hard, he choked.

He summoned Gladys on instinct, forgetting about the protection spell around the clearing in his panic, and launched her toward the woman. Gladys hit the invisible barrier again, and this time, she didn't bounce back into Virgil's hand; she fell to the ground and rolled away, as if she were dazed.

"Oh. Right," Virgil said.

The woman in the cloak reached up and touched the purple pendant around her throat. It began to glow with a deep light of shadow magic. Her mouth moved as she recited a dark spell.

"Simon!" Virgil cried over his shoulder. "Help?"

But Simon was still lying on the ground, dazed and only just beginning to get his bearings.

Virgil's whole body tensed. He powered up his hands, and they glowed with bright orange light. He stood with his knees bent, his legs cocked like springs, ready for whatever the woman could throw at him.

Or so he hoped.

The pendant grew brighter and brighter in her hands, and her lips moved quicker and quicker. Suddenly, the light trail in the sky above them retracted, shrinking away from the city of Templar and reeling back to the energy column that shot up from the Refracticore.

Virgil looked up and gazed at the rapidly-shortening light trail in confusion. Then he looked back down at the woman in the purple cloak. She wasn't frowning anymore; now she was grinning, a sharp, dangerous smile that sent a chill through Virgil's heart. She let go of the pendant, and he saw that the purple light had transferred to her hands, which glowed from the palms. She raised her hands into the air, held them above her head for two seconds, and then she brought them crashing down, both slicing through the air, throwing the purple shadow-light to the ground.

The sky above Virgil opened up, and a brilliant, white energy column surged down on him from above.

Virgil threw up his hands, forming shields against the heat and light, but the Refracticore's power was far greater than his own, and the energy column smashed through both kinesthetic barriers as if they had been made of brittle glass. The powerful electricity crashed down on him like a wave.

All he could do was scream.

CHAPTER 28

Simon's vision cleared, and the forest filtered back into focus. He looked up and saw Virgil staring toward the Refracticore.

Then a surging column of energy flashed down from the sky and consumed his friend in a blinding-white deluge of scorching heat and pain.

"Virgil!" Simon screamed, pushing himself to his feet. He didn't think, he just acted on pure instinct. He flicked his fingers as he ran forward, and a shield appeared in his hand. He threw the disc like a Frisbee, straight into the path of the energy column, above Virgil's head, but as soon as it hit the crackling white light, the orange magic fizzled and disintegrated into nothingness.

Simon charged forward, holding out his arms and forming a kinesthetic plow with his hands, and he plunged toward Virgil, trying to knock him free of the lightning column's grip. But the plow cracked and splintered when it hit the light, and then *it* disintegrated, too. Simon nearly went head-first into the life-draining electricity and just barely pulled himself back in time.

"Virgil!" he screamed again, but if Virgil could hear him through the surge of power that was sucking out his youth, he didn't show it. Simon watched with horror through the veil of white-hot light as Virgil's skin began to grow dry and cracked, and a streak of his hair began to fade from brown to silver.

Simon's howl of rage shook the leaves on the trees around him.

He turned toward the Refracticore, and for the first time, he saw the woman in the purple cloak standing across the clearing.

An anger that he had never known caught fire in his chest and burned through his entire body.

He stomped toward the clearing, firing a stream of bright energy blasts at the woman. The balls of bright orange light were wild, uncontrolled, and filled with fury, but they moved like homing missiles, swerving around the elderly energy-suckers, dodging the Refracticore, and screeching straight at the woman, a steady barrage of powerful magic blasts. The Refracticore managed to fend off about half of the shots, zapping out thin bolts of purple electricity and disintegrating the magic orbs as they flew through the air. The other half did make it across the clearing, but the stone in the woman's necklace glowed brightly and formed a translucent purple shadow-shield around her. The energy blasts collided with the shield and dissipated, leaving the woman unharmed.

The fire in Simon's belly raged. He threw more and more blasts, his arms pumping like pistons, firing shot after shot after shot after shot. But every single attack was either thwarted by the Refracticore or evaporated by her shield, and after almost thirty straight seconds of firing a furious flurry of attacks, Simon was out of breath, his arms were tired, and the woman was completely unharmed.

And her smile…her cold, cruel, vicious smile remained.

Simon felt the heat of Virgil's energy column on his back. He turned to look at his friend. Even through the glare of the electricity, he could tell that Virgil's fingernails were turning yellow and brittle. The people in the clearing were sucking the life out of him, all at the same time, and he was going fast.

If an individual lightning bolt from the Refracticore's energy beam could drain a healthy teenager into a barely-breathing corpse in less than an hour…and if eight lightning bolts could kill a football player in just a few minutes…then a full-bore energy column sucking out his youth meant that Virgil only had seconds to live.

Simon didn't know what to do.

He switched off his mind. He let the power inside him take over.

Instinctively, he knew that fighting the woman would do no good. Even if he managed to take her out, she wasn't the immediate threat; the Refracticore was. Though revenge against the mysterious woman for everything she'd wrought might be cathartic, it wouldn't stop the evil gemstone from draining his friend's life and redistributing it to a group of craven, selfish octogenarians. It wouldn't save Virgil. And even though she had no magic of her own, she seemed to be protected by the shadow-creature's magic that lived within her necklace; forcing his way through a black magic that powerful would be a waste of time.

So he focused on the Refracticore.

Virgil had found in his research that the stone was indestructible. Simon clenched his jaw.

He was going to test that theory to its limit.

All of these calculations were made within the flash of an instant. Simon raised his arms, pointing his open hands directly at the Refracticore gem. His anger and terror and helplessness exploded within him, like an all-consuming atomic blast, and he screamed as he fired two steady columns of powerful orange magic from his palms. Like the streams from two flamethrowers, the magic surged forward, slicing the space between two of the elderly figures and streaming straight at the Refracticore. Simon put every ounce of magical force he could into the power blasting out from his hands. The gold of the Refracticore's staff began to glow red with the heat of his fire.

He blasted the magic until he had no more to give, and when the stream of energy trailed off, Simon sank to his knees, exhausted by the effort. He looked up at the Refracticore stone.

It still sat in its mounting, strong and whole, still firing out golden youth-energy bursts to the people in the clearing.

"No!" Simon bellowed. He dug his knees into the earth, and he thrust his hands into the dirt, pressing his fingers down into the soil, past the roots of the grass, into the heart of the mud. He screamed with all of his fury, and he sent a reserve energy he didn't know existed down into the ground. All around the clearing, small, green tendrils burst through the groundcover, twirling and unrolling as they grew into hundreds of stout green stalks. Each stalk bloomed with a fist-sized aqua-marine flower, and all of the petals from the flowers opened at the same time. Small, orange spheres the size of ball bearings floated up around the trees as they were released from the flowers like spores. The orbs floated upward a few feet, until they were suspended above the ground at the same height as the Refracticore…and then, in a furious onslaught, they pinged across the clearing, cracking into the gemstone like a hailstorm from all sides. The forest filled with the hard sounds of metal cracking against diamond, *tat-tat-tat-tat-tat*, like machine gun fire.

When the flurry of ball bearings subsided, the balls fell to the ground, where they sank back down into the dirt, to once again become one with the earth…and the Refracticore gem remained unharmed.

"No," Simon whispered softly, shaking his head in disbelief.

He collapsed forward as all strength and hope evaporated from his body. His chest heaved as his lungs clawed desperately for breath, and every muscle in his body burned with exhaustion. The soft dirt felt cool against his burning skin. He raised his weary eyes to the energy column and to his best friend, trapped inside and being drained of his life. The silver streak in his hair had extended to full white, and the rest was beginning to pepper in with silver. His arms were shrinking, the muscle draining off of his bones, and his skin was so dry that it was practically translucent. Wrinkles pinched at the corners of his eyes, and Simon watched as one of his friend's teeth fell out of his gums.

Tears streamed down Simon's cheeks. "I'm sorry," he whispered.

Then something in the foreground of his vision caught his eye.

Simon pushed himself up to his knees. He crawled forward, staring down at Virgil's wooden curiocus ball.

And suddenly, the answer was simple.

Simon grinned.

He knew how to defeat the Refracticore.

He dredged up the little strength he had left and hauled himself to his feet. He swayed like a punch-drunk boxer, trying to keep his footing. The woman in the cloak had been watching his magical onslaught with interest bordering on awe, and she watched him carefully now, from her perch near the van. The Refracticore continued its awful distribution of Virgil's power, and judging by the looks of the old folks around the circle, its work was almost done.

Everything seemed to move in slow motion for Simon as he approached the clearing one final time.

He held up his hand and called up every drop of magic he had left. A kinesthetic shield formed in his palm, small, and thin, and weak. He hoped it would be enough. It was all the magic he had left.

He closed his eyes in concentration as he walked toward the circle, his shield held out before him. He crossed into the clearing, and the Refracticore fired a purple energy blast his way. He opened his eyes just in time to see it, and he moved his hand, blocking the shot. It took a chip out of his shield, but the structure held. He continued forward, walking straight toward the gemstone. The Refracticore fired more shots, and he caught those, too. His shield cracked, then it split in half. He used the last of his mental strength to hold the two pieces of the shield together. He just needed a few more seconds…

The Refracticore attacked more ferociously as he approached, but Simon pushed on. He sidestepped some of the energy bolts, while others hit the shield and broke it into more and more pieces. He was barely holding the orange surface together. A few more hits, and the shield would disintegrate. He needed to move faster, but his body was so tired…

He trudged forward. The woman in the cloak watched him with interest, clearly wondering why he would choose this particular method of suicide. It did occur to Simon that that's exactly what this might end up being, if he couldn't reach the Refracticore in time.

But if he died, he would die trying to save his best friend.

And, he figured, there were worse ways to go.

He took another step. The Refracticore fired another shot; this one shattered the shield into a thousand tiny shards that exploded out from his hand and rained down on the ground like bits of broken glass. Simon's legs gave out beneath him, and with his last ounce of strength, he pitched himself forward. He reached out with one hand, and just as the Refracticore shot out one final purple bolt of deadly, malignant power, Simon's hand brushed the refracted surface of the gemstone…

And then the Refracticore was gone. Vanished into thin air.

The energy blast reaching up into the sky dissipated instantly. The purple clouds cleared, and the shortened light trail evaporated, along with the energy column that was consuming Virgil. In a split second, all the energy and power and lightning and magic dematerialized from the space, and there was nothing left but a ring of now-young people gathered around an empty golden staff.

Simon collapsed, hitting the ground with a hard thud. Exhaustion wracked his body, and the world began to swim out of focus. The last thing he saw before he lost consciousness was the woman in the purple cloak ushering the residents of Furtive Hills back into the van and jumping into the driver's seat, revving the engine and tearing away down the bumpy path.

A heavy curtain fell over Simon then, and as he drifted into darkness, he smiled.

CHAPTER 29

"What…happened?"

Virgil came to on the wet, dewy grass, alone near the edge of the clearing, surrounded by the dark of the nighttime forest.

His eyes had a hard time adjusting to the dim light, and his memory was fuzzy. He remembered the woman in the purple cloak…he remembered a bright flash of white…and he remembered pain.

An awful, unbearable pain.

"Simon?" he asked. But he couldn't see through the trees.

He placed a hand against a tree trunk and used it to help himself up to his feet. His bones ached, and his entire body was trembling. He felt as dry as a desert, and everything popped and cracked when he moved.

He stumbled forward on shaky legs, toward the clearing where the Refracticore had stood, sucking up his energy and transferring it to the assembled group. That was only…minutes ago? Hours ago? Days ago? He had no sense of time. But the clearing was empty now.

As he stumbled into the open circle, he realized that wasn't entirely true. The gold staff remained, still stuck into the earth. And next to it lay Simon, collapsed in a disastrous heap.

"Simon!"

Virgil hurried forward, losing his footing and crashing to the ground next to his friend. Something cracked in his hip, and he felt a sting, but nothing felt broken. He pushed the small pain away and reached out, turning Simon onto his back. He patted his friend's face, trying to wake him up. "Simon?"

Simon's eyes fluttered open. He looked over at Virgil.

He smiled.

"What happened?" Virgil asked, helping Simon up to a seat.

Simon brushed himself off and raised himself carefully to his feet, then he pulled Virgil up after him. Simon inspected his friend in the moonlight, and he frowned. "You got old," he said.

Virgil touched his face, and he winced at the papery feel of his skin. "I *thought* I felt different," he said miserably. He reached into his pocket and pulled out his phone. He turned on the camera and took a picture of his face, blinding himself with the flash. Once the bright spots had cleared from his vision, he focused on the image, and he gasped. "I look like an *adult!*" he said.

Simon couldn't help but laugh. The moonlight had been a little deceiving, and in the brightness of the camera flash, he saw that Virgil wasn't quite as far gone as he seemed at first. His skin was dry and would need some serious attention…he had wrinkles around his eyes that were probably there to stay. "You're going to need some moisturizer," Simon said, and he couldn't suppress a grin. "Probably a little calcium for those old bones."

"I hate milk," Virgil groaned. "It makes my mouth all gummy."

"Your hair is probably beyond hope."

"I think the streak makes me look distinguished. And I think I'm missing a tooth…"

"You should probably see a doctor."

"Yeah, I'm going to Urgent Care tomorrow," Virgil agreed.

Simon reached out and gave his friend a hug. He couldn't help it.

"All right, all right," Virgil said, clapping Simon on the back. "But seriously. What happened?"

"I realized I couldn't destroy the Refracticore," Simon said. Then, before Virgil could say anything, he added, "Just like Reddit said, I know, I know."

"Reddit knows everything," Virgil grinned.

"I couldn't destroy it, so I didn't," Simon continued with a shrug.

Virgil looked around suspiciously. "You didn't destroy it… but it's not here anymore," he observed.

"Correct. I couldn't destroy it, so instead, I locked it away." Simon allowed himself an immensely satisfied grin. His face beamed with pride as he said, "The Refracticore is locked away in my psychic vault."

Virgil's eyes narrowed. "I'm sorry, it's *what?*"

"It's in my vault," Simon repeated, the grin now spreading into a full smile. "I threw everything I had at that stupid rock. I mean, *everything*. You wouldn't believe…well, I'll tell you about that later. But in the end, I realized I didn't *have* to destroy it, I just had to remove it from the situation. So I opened my vault, walked up to the stone, put my hand on it, closed my eyes, imagined I was in front of the vault—"

"—and the Refracticore was there in your hand, just like Gladys, or your key," Virgil said with awe.

Simon nodded. "Yep. I figured if it works with those magic objects, maybe it'll work with other magic objects, too. And it did."

Virgil shook his head in wonder. "Wow."

"So I threw the Refracticore inside, slammed the door, and locked it. I am now the proud owner of an indestructible, dark-magic Refracticore."

Virgil frowned. "Well is it still…you know…refracticoring? What's going to happen when you open the vault again?"

Simon hadn't thought about that. He furrowed his brow. "I guess we'll see," he finally decided.

Virgil looked around the clearing. "And the Cocoon Club?" Virgil asked. "They just…left?"

"Yeah," Simon nodded. "I kind of blacked out, but the last

thing I saw was the woman in the cloak getting everyone in the van and tearing off. I…think I might have freaked her out. There were fire streams and attack flowers," he explained.

"So she's still on the loose," Virgil sighed.

"She is," Simon confirmed. "But we know she's connected to Furtive Hills, whatever that is. If we can find that, we can find her. Think you can connect with that guy on Reddit who posted about the van disappearing?"

Virgil gasped. "I thought you'd never ask."

"If we find Furtive Hills, we find her. And if we find her, we might find this shadow…thing."

"Shadow *Lord*," Virgil informed him.

Simon raised an eyebrow. "Shadow Lord?"

Virgil nodded. "That's his name. I decided."

Simon sighed. He was too tired to argue. "Okay, so if we find her, we might find the Shadow Lord. And if we find him…maybe we can stop the darkness from taking over Templar."

"He does seem to have his fingers in a lot of pies," Virgil observed.

"First Neil, now this…who knows what else—or *who* else—he's controlling."

"And Neil isn't the only one that he's 'chosen,'" Virgil pointed out. "We can pretty much bet all these not-quite-so-old-any-more folks are solidly on his side."

Simon nodded slowly, turning all these thoughts over in his mind. "Well," he finally said, "this is a discussion for another day, when you're in full health, and when we have a wizard back on our side."

"Oh, right. Llewyn's an ice cube," Virgil grimaced.

"Maybe not. Let's head back and see if Abby had any luck summoning Morgaine."

"Okay," Virgil agreed. They started back toward their car,

Virgil leaning heavily on Simon as they hobbled through the dark woods. It was slow going, but they didn't mind—darkness or no darkness, it was nice to be outside, in the fresh air, without the threat of a new piece of scorched earth lurking on the horizon. "Hey," Virgil said, giving Simon's shoulder a squeeze, "by the way…thanks for saving my life."

Simon smiled. "No need to thank me," he said. "It's just what a hero does."

"It's what a friend does, too," Virgil said.

Simon smiled at that.

CHAPTER 30

Abby cleared her throat. *Here we go*, she thought.

The tent flap lifted, and Simon and Virgil ducked into the mansion. They stepped into the light, and Abby gasped. "Virgil! What *happened?*"

Virgil turned to Simon and frowned. "She doesn't think I look distinguished," he said.

"What can I say?" Simon asked with a shrug. "You're not everyone's taste."

"I assume you'll give me a full rundown later?" Abby asked weakly, crooking an eyebrow. She was still wracked by the poison-fever, and when she thought about it again, she didn't have the energy for one of Virgil's explanations.

"Later," Virgil confirmed. "But everything's good. Promise."

"Well," Abby said, measuring her words. "I wouldn't necessarily say *that*."

"What do you mean?" Simon asked.

Abby took a deep breath. "You know how I said I'd find a way to summon Morgaine."

"Right…" Virgil said suspiciously.

"Okay, well…everything's frozen, so…you know, I wasn't sure how to find more information. So I wandered around a little, and I went into the potions room, and there was this thing in the corner called a spell sponge. Have you ever heard of a spell sponge?"

"No," Simon said.

"We're new at this," Virgil explained.

Abby cleared her throat uncomfortably. She wasn't quite sure how to explain everything, and her brain was still feeling fuzzy, which wasn't helping matters. So she just started talking.

"Well, okay. So a spell sponge is this thing...it's a sponge, basically, like a bath sponge. But instead of water, it soaks up magic. Which I'm guessing is why Llewyn had one in the potions room, so he could clean up any magic potion spills. So there was one in there, and the thing about it is, even if it's frozen, it still works. It'll still suck up the magic, as long as the magic itself isn't frozen. And if you'll recall, there is exactly one thing of Llewyn's in this mansion that didn't freeze when he did."

"The red letters," Simon said with sudden realization. He hadn't even considered that before, but the red paste on the wall hadn't formed into letters until *after* Llewyn had frozen. "Whatever he used was still...I don't know...*active*."

Abby nodded. "Right. So I used the sponge and soaked up the words. Then I wrung the thing out, and the red liquid dripped onto the floor. I did it just in case maybe Llewyn had planned for this, and had put *more* magic inside his magic. And it turns out...he did."

Virgil screwed up his face in confusion. "I'm going to go ahead and say that I understand what you're saying, but I want to make it clear that I do not."

"It doesn't really matter," Abby said dismissively, pushing back a lock of purple hair that had fallen into her eyes. "The point is, the potion or paste or whatever that he had used to make the words 'summon Morgaine' hit the floor, and they made new words. And *those* words gave me step-by-step instructions on how to summon her."

"So Morgaine is a her?" Simon asked. "That's part of the mystery solved, at least."

"She's not just a her," Abby sighed. "I think she's *her*."

Simon furrowed his brow. "I might be too tired for this conversation, but I don't know what that means."

Abby clicked her teeth together thoughtfully. "She goes by other names," she finally said. "You...might know one or two of them."

Virgil squinted suspiciously. "Who is it?" he asked.

Abby didn't know quite know how to put it. "Look, let's just say, I'm a little confused about why Llewyn would have asked us to bring her here. You should see for yourself, but...she's dangerous. I mean, *dangerous*. And for him to ask us to bring her into his house...I have to imagine that she is literally the only person who can free him from the ice. Otherwise, he's put us all at extraordinary risk for nothing."

Simon found himself squirming. "Well...what if we *don't* summon her?" he asked. "I mean, maybe she *is* the only person who can set him free, but maybe we should exhaust every other option first. Really make sure, you know?"

Abby pressed her fingers to her forehead and rubbed her temples hard. "It...might be too late for that," she said.

Virgil started. "Did you already summon her? On your own?"

Abby frowned. "I didn't know what else to do," she said.

Simon looked around the mansion's sitting room. "Where is she?" he asked. "Is she working on Llewyn? Is she back there with him?" He started walking toward the back hall, and Virgil followed.

"Not *exactly*," Abby said, hurrying to keep up with their long strides.

"What does that mean?" Simon asked, walking faster as a strange panic started to creep up in his chest. He climbed over the rubble in the hallway and pushed through the door. "Abby, what are you—?"

He stepped through the doorway, and he froze. He gaped down the hall at the thing that now filled the space between the walls, just past the frozen figure of Llewyn.

It was a long, narrow box hammered together from heavy, ancient wood—a coffin, old and worn, and bound with four different chains, each one heavier than the last. They were secured with heavy, rusted padlocks, and in case the chains weren't enough to hold whatever creature was inside, the whole casket had been tied shut with a thick, winding rope, and all the seams in the coffin had been sealed with thick red wax.

Simon gasped as he read the true name of the woman inside, which was scratched into the surface of the weathered wood.

"Guys," Abby said awkwardly, gesturing toward the box, "I just summoned Morgan le Fay."

SIMON AND VIRGIL WILL RETURN IN:

SHADOW REALM

BOOK THREE OF
THE DARK MATTER SERIES

A NOTE FROM THE AUTHOR

If you enjoyed this book, please take a moment to leave a review on Amazon. Reviews really do make or break the success of a book for independent authors, and your support would be truly and greatly appreciated.

ABOUT THE AUTHOR

Clayton Smith is an award-winning Midwestern writer who once erroneously referred to himself as a "national treasure." He is the author of several novels, short story collections, and plays, including the best-selling Apocalypticon series. His short fiction has been featured in national literary journals, including Canyon Voices and Write City Magazine.

He is also rather tall.

Find him online StateOfClayton.com and on social media as @Claytonsaurus.

www.ingramcontent.com/pod-product-compliance
Lightning Source LLC
Chambersburg PA
CBHW050344030726
47503CB00008B/2614